ALL THE DAYS OF THE WEEK

Angela Dutra de Menezes

ALL THE DAYS OF THE WEEK

1st Edition
POD

Petrópolis
KBR
2012

Text edition **Alan Sklar**
Translation **Fal Vitiello**
Cover **Tatiana Marotta**

ISBN: 978-85-8180-023-3

KBR Editora Digital Ltda.
www.kbrdigital.com.br
atendimento@kbrdigital.com.br
55|24|2222.3491

B869 - Brazilian Literature

Printed in Brazil

Angela Dutra de Menezes is a Brazilian writer and journalist. She was born in Rio de Janeiro, where she still lives. She worked at *O Globo* and on the weekly magazine *Veja*. She wrote *A Thousand Years Minus Fifty* (1995), *Saint Sofia* (1997)—considered in Spain one of the 5 best novels of the year 1997—*The Other Side Of The Picture* (1998) and *The Book of Apocalypses According To A Witness* (2001). In 2000 she published the collection of essays *The Portuguese That Gaves Us Birth*—one of the 10 best books of the year according to *O Globo*. *All The Days Of The Week* is her first book of short stories and her first book translated into English.

Email: angela.dutra@terra.com.br

ACKNOWLEDGMENTS

To my siblings, Iau and Lula
who each in their own time,
left too early,
taking a lot of me with them.

TABLE OF CONTENTS

Sunday

Since youth, when he used to dream of flying saucer crew members dictating messages to him in incomprehensible languages, Edmundo Santos Fogaça dedicated all his free time to the study of Ufology. In his accounting office, he accumulated piles and piles of documented evidence of the alien's invasion of the serene routine of our humble planet. From analyzed photographs—of which there was no chance of forgery, since they had a security seal affixed by NASA to the recorded tapes with the incomprehensible language— identified, but not decoded, though Fogaça had researched thousands of publications in countless libraries.

Finally, his tireless efforts were gloriously rewarded. It was a language of the Orion family, specifically of the Lacteous branch—information that he had found in an old dictionary edited in the extinct Soviet Union, one of the triumphs of the Galactic infiltration; Stalin himself was actually a disguised alien, of noble origin, by the way. Fogaça made sure to emphasize Stalin had been born of the Sagittarius line, under the star *Eta Carinae*, in the Nebula of the same name.

"Wow, he must have had trouble sending a letter to his mother," joked one of his friends, which caused the end of the friendship. Edmundo Santos Fogaça could never accept playful comments regarding such an important subject. After insulting the mediocre ex-friend, who could only see the obvious, Fogaça added:

"Poor terrestrial man, you are nothing but an amoeba. You need to learn how to listen, as Jesus taught. He was an alien ahead of his times, worshipped and adored and nobody dared to doubt or analyze his powers, which were miraculous gifts from the peoples of the universe. If you studied a little before saying idiocies you would know that Stalin belonged to a race that has wandered space for millennia, looking for new harbors, no longer able to deal with the excess of their population."

The unshakable faith in sidereal civilizations, all with the fixed objective of conquering the Earth, forced him to remove himself from the daily habits of normal people—going to the beach or to the cinema, reading, dancing, and listening to music for instance. Besides other Ufologists, Fogaça had no friends. His life was limited to his work as a free-lance accountant and the planetary-metaphysical research. There was no detail about flying saucers, humanoids or aliens, living among us in disguise—learning our ways to eventually conquer us— which he did not know about. In spite of the disbelief of some of his peers, Fogaça had even met the Varginha Alien himself, having conversed with him several times—telepathically, of course. Fogaça had never learned Lacteous-Oranian, and the Varginha Alien could not speak Portuguese, although Fogaça could have sworn that, after tasting the traditional "*doce de leite*"[1] from Minas Gerais, the alien was unable to look at a

---

1 Typical dessert from the State of Minas Gerais, with milk and sugar.

cow without saying, "*Trem bão, sô.*"[2]

Following a well-organized and boring routine, Fogaça waited for Sundays with obvious emotion. Year after year, just after sunrise, he would travel from Rio to Petrópolis, a city in the mountains. There, on the top of the Retiro Hill, there was a landing field for alien ships, where he would stay for 24 hours, waiting for a miracle—who knows, they could come to abduct him! Fogaça would bet all his fortune, in Ramil,[3] that an extraordinarily large mother ship travelled around the Earth and would soon release her daughter ships to save those who believed in a larger life, a life beautiful enough to go beyond this shitty little planet, lost in the universe, from impending apocalypse. Those who knew better would say, that only terrestrial scum could cultivate the vanity of seeing their world as the center of the universe. It was about that subject and other topics—invariably, cosmonautic gossip—that Fogaça and the other regular visitors of the landing field would speak, while they waited for the *Close Encounter of the Third Kind*—seeing flesh and bone (or whatever material they were made of) aliens, face to face. The *Close Encounter of the Third Kind* seemed to be a dream—it never happened. However, on a chilly night, Fogaça and two friends had the honor and the privilege of hearing the conversation of an alien couple. According to the insiders, the trio also had made the equally rare *Close Encounter of the Second Kind*, a true apotheosis. Unfortunately, they could not understand what the couple said, or how they had appeared on the hill. For hours, they searched the splendid blue of the winter night, but there was not one single spaceship in the sky. Suddenly, out of nowhere the aliens appeared. The evidence

---

2 Popular expression in Minas Gerais meaning "This is awesome."
3 Currency used in Vulcano, planet hidden by the Mercury orbit and inhabited by humanoids with asbestos bodies.

of the fact—Fogaça took pictures of them and recorded their conversation—generated months of discussions and a thesis published on the famous London newspaper *New Age News.*

Signed by Edmundo dos Santos Fogaça, the revolutionary discovery, documented in beautiful photographs, supported with a meretricious narrative that alien beings were made of human matter, and that—surprise!—the male had something similar to the flu—between grunts, he sniffed and panted until he fell, almost breathless, on top of his female companion, who rocked him gently until he could stand up again. As Fogaça skillfully wrote in his conclusion to the article, through the immeasurable competence of Brazilian Ufologists, they had obtained proof of the soul that lived inside those strange bodies—a proof they had been searching for centuries: "(...) *there is no reason to fear our sidereal brothers, they have the feelings of superior spirits. I have seen it with my own eyes, the female was extremely tender.*"

Even with the sensation caused in the international esoteric communities—East and West inviting Fogaça, the new expert in interplanetary metaphysics, to attend debates and conferences—the best result of this spectacular field research was his marriage to a shop assistant who worked in the photo place where he had the sensational films developed. A beautiful, charming brunette, Magda da Conceição had been taken aback when she looked at the photos—*well, well, who could have imagined?* The moment Fogaça showed up to pick up the photos, she shook her shoulders, flashing the sure smile of those who have just hit their target:

"So! What a surprise Mr. Fogaça! Have you given up on the aliens? That was unexpected, you and your attitude, with a weak spot for dirty pictures..."

Edmundo Santos Fogaça did not waste his time with ignorant people who were incapable of seeing the beauty in the occult. Explaining to that poor girl the scientific importance of what she had in her hands? Imagine that. Despite his irritation with such stupidity—the girl could see sex in the most serious discovery ever made by Mankind —something powerful kept him chained to the photo shop. Standing before Magda, he analyzed every angle of the pioneer work, solemnly ignoring the curious comments:

"My God, I have never done anything like this! Jesus, Mr. Fogaça, are you a pervert? Look, what a well-endowed alien! Are you going to sell the pictures to porn sites?"

The scientific soul of Edmundo Santos Fogaça could not take the offense. He looked at the shop assistant, ready to confront her; to call the manager; to ask that she was immediately fired. But he ended up drowning in the waves of her eyes, two emerald drops, shining with mischief, with life, with intent. To make the story short, they were married within the year—both madly in love. She knew well her husband's manias, but was willing to accept them. She did not believe any of the foolish theories researched by Fogaça, but the man was worthy. He was kind, generous, sweet and funny, and honored his name by being the perfect lover. On his part, he accepted the total absence of neurons in his wife's head. In his opinion, Magda was just like the majority of terrestrials—nothing but a fool who could see only what was before her eyes. Theirs was, ideologically and philosophically, the perfect marriage; the spouses knew each other's flaws, and that match could never fail.

And indeed, it did not fail. Madga brought some joy to the black-and-white life of the star accountant. She organized his papers, the boxes and boxes of photos and documents about UFOs, abductions and creepy stories. To lighten up the atmosphere of the office, heavy and suffocating with all those mysteries, she had set up the files, correlating incidents according to the events that Mankind was going through when they had occurred.

That was how the "Alien DOI-CODI"[4] came to be a common visitor during the 1970's. The Pele abduction had happened in 1958. Magda called Saddam a 2003 alien of unpredictable habits—he came and went without logic—, a name that her husband's friends, equally nuts, immediately adopted.

"Sorry I'm late, traffic problems. Has Saddam showed up?"

"Not yet. But the spaceship flew by twice."

Not even his *Close Encounter of the Second Kind*, for which Fogaça was honored as a *Scientist Of Super And Sublunary Astrophysics*, escaped Magda's irony. Laughing, she named the event "Fellatio." The envelope with the evidence and the souvenirs from the event that had shaken modern thinking had actually been named after this vulgar expression, and Fogaça was angered. After much debate, they chose a more suitable word, appropriate to the importance of the famous researcher. Deep inside, Fogaça liked Magda's reckless lightness—if she did not believe, at least she was sincere and had a good sense of humor. God forbid his own wife should make fun of him behind his back.

Until she became pregnant with their first child—a boy they named Hubble, after the telescope, Magda always accompanied Fogaça on the weekly trips to the landing field in Petrópolis. She took fruit, cans of beer, boiled eggs—changing the study meeting into a picnic. When Asdrúbal Penaforte, a retired doctor who was the leader of the Ufologists, com-

---

4 Investigation Government Department during the military dictatorship in Brazil.

plained about the heresy—*if that went on, the research meeting would end up in a party*—Magda explained:

"First of all, Dr. Asdrúbal, if the aliens come, we must welcome them with kindness, showing them we are friends. Besides, I don't think they will take long. I think they will come from one of the hundred extra-solar planets we have evidence of. I personally think our contact will be made with someone from HD 209458B, which orbits the star HD 209458, very similar to the Sun and only 150 light years away from the Earth. You know that HD 209458B is located in the Pegasus constellation, don't you?"

Thank God, Saddam had not finished his landing maneuvers yet and escaped the commotion. Everyone was flabbergasted, including Fogaça. Saddam would also be affected by this sudden, weird knowledge exhibited by Magda. Not even Asdrúbal's medicine would save the alien, an organism that was not fond of oxygen, if he went into shock with these extraordinary words of the young Mrs. Fogaça, a beautiful home keeper who nobody took seriously. When she stopped talking, Magda saw her husband's pride and the surprised expression on the others' faces. From that day on, they started to consider her one of them. But there were those who believed there was more to her—*Magda was actually an alien.*

Magda took advantage of that fact and had a lot of fun. Every now and then, without warning, she said something that would cause a fuss. Fogaça was having a ball; he knew she was just joking, but the rest of the gang was breathless—how could a simple girl, who was nothing more than a shop assistant before she married Fogaça, know so many details about noble interstellar protocol? On the following Sunday, without asking Fogaça's permission, a group decided to force her to explain the source of that knowledge. She did not think twice:

"Fogaça teaches me. Come on, I ask, he answers. You seem to forget that my husband is a genius, respected all over the world—in all worlds. I know, for instance, that Saddam is not coming today. The core of his planet was severely reduced and made life impossible. Poor Saddam, he lived in an inhabitable star system. As you surely are aware, planets evaporate when they are less than seven million kilometers away from a star. Its radiation disperses hydrogen and there isn't a single planetary mass that can resist a leak of 100 km/second. Would anyone like a sandwich—a piece of cake?"

And so it was. The excess of knowledge defined Magda, who undoubtedly belonged to the class of the *sent ones*, the inquisitors concluded. To explain further, though Magda was unaware of the fact, she was part of an *Advanced Order*—groups from other spheres, transported to Earth to understand it and conquer it. Fogaça's wife, the geniuses of the group quickly concluded, did not belong to the human race. It actually made sense. Fogaça, the best among the best, had probably married the great-grand-daughter of Stalin, a deserved award for such an expert in UFOs and aliens.

"*Habemus* alien," said Dr. Asdrúbal, looking at Magda's ass. *What an ass*, he thought; *it is worth waiting for others like that, so round, to fall from the sky, right on top of his head.*

When she heard the comments, Magda did not hesitate, she started to learn Russian. On Sundays, when she arrived at the landing field, she greeted the friends in an offhanded manner:

"*Dóbray útra*. I mean, good morning."

And she went on her way smiling, indifferent to the surprise she caused with her linguistic slip. As they started to forget her, Saddam would return to the center of the debate— *could he have vaporized just like his planet?* Magda spoke something in Russian and they looked at her with astonished interest again. She repeated so many *"spaassiba"*—when she meant thank you; so many *"des vidania"*—to say goodbye— and *"pajalsta"*—as a sign of gratitude, that one fine day Asdrúbal made an announcement. He said that the Brazilian Ufology Society,[5] during a secret meeting in which he had the honor of participating, representing Petrópolis and the deceased Saddam, had decided that Magda would be the subject of a rigorous study, due to her surprising knowledge of the cosmos and her alarming command of the Soviet language. Magda's green eyes became larger—she made an innocent face and protested:

"*Ya ni gavariu pa Russki.* I mean, I can't speak Russian."

Fogaça, the scientist, a brilliant and devout man who dedicated his life to the search for wanderers of the sky, reacted like any hot-blooded South-American macho:

"Let's not mix friendship with business. She's my wife and nobody touches her, end of story!"

Divine Providence never fails. Before Fogaça had the chance to argue with his old friends, and before disorder reigned down among the researchers, Magda got pregnant and stopped accompanying her husband on the Sunday trips. She said that the smell of spaceship fuel made her morning sickness worse. Fogaça almost died laughing.

"You're incorrigible. Do you think I believe that? But it's a good excuse."

To be fair, Magda's absence reduced the charm of the vigils in Petrópolis. No more coffee; no more sandwiches; no more cakes, sweets and fruit; and especially, no more joy— for Magda could always make a funny comment out of the

---

5 Non-profit entity, with the right of vote in the Space Galactic Confederation.

blue. The hours seemed to take longer to pass. Even the aliens showed their discontent and started to come less and less often. Sometimes a spaceship gave signs of life and the Ufologists went crazy. They forgot about Magda and engaged in exciting discussions: who the aliens were; where they came from; if they finally would dare to make direct contact.

Meanwhile, in Rio, Magda behaved in an irreprehensible manner. She woke up late; watched television; spent the whole day alone. The neighbors talked about how lucky Fogaça was, that raving mad lunatic—the flying saucer hunter who went after aliens with a butterfly net had married a young woman who was honorable, beautiful and friendly. "She is too good for him," said the building administrator, with an ironic tone. She disliked Fogaça and her feelings were returned—he hated her.

But it was the building administrator who helped Magda when Hubble decided to be born on a Sunday. When he came back home, on Monday, with lots of stories to tell—they had almost had another *Encounter of the Second Kind* but the aliens were scared off by Asdrúbal's sneezing—Fogaça bumped right into the angry lady, who was waiting for him at the door:

"What a shame, Mr. Fogaça! While you were playing hide and seek with the aliens, your beautiful wife gave birth to a boy. They are both very well, thanks to God and to me, who took her to the hospital in time. Now, try to get some sense, because you're an adult and you have a son to raise."

After Hubble's birth, the routine changed. Too busy with the little heir, Magda never returned to the landing field again, and lost interest in Fogaça's files. But one day, hearing him talk about the scare they had with a spaceship that almost crashed into the Rio-Petrópolis highway, she seemed to relive the old times. She blinked those green eyes and asked her husband to tell her about the episode in detail.

In the hope of seeing his wife keeping him company again and coloring his Sundays with her spirit, Fogaça exaggerated the details of the golden lights of the spaceship, its maneuvers trying to land with the grace of a bird, until the dramatic moment when the UFO shook, recovered its elegance, stabilized and disappeared. Feigning indifference, Magda declared:

"That was not a spaceship, Fogaça. What you are describing is a flying drag queen, falling from her high heels."

That was the last participation Magda ever had in her husband's research. From that day on, when she was not pregnant, she was breast-feeding. She only remembered the aliens when the children were born and Fogaça gave them preposterous names: Hubble, Zeta Grey and Moth; three green-eyed boys, Magda's green eyes, emerald waves with magnetic attraction. Despite the distance from his wife, who had become more and more disconnected from the alien business, Fogaça was a happy man. He never noticed Magda's irritation with the lack of money, for he had abandoned his accountancy office— he lived exclusively to track and search the ends of the nebulas. He could only see the mess he was in one Monday, when he returned from Petrópolis and found a note on the table:

On Sunday, the ships are coming to the planet Earth. I will go with the children. One day, perhaps I will return to this world. Be happy. Magda.

Fogaça was desperate. He could never forgive himself for having stopped Asdrúbal from studying the woman—all that grace, those eyes, her strong and honest attitude. Only Fogaça, the famous scientist, had not noticed that his wife was an alien in disguise.

He never had the courage to tell the truth to the Ufologists in Petrópolis; he had spent the last 10 years having a *Close Encounter of the Third Kind*. No human being had ever accomplished that before, and Fogaça, as any other husband, had not seen the miracle. Tortured by guilt, he kept his vigil at the landing field—he did not stop to rest for one second, always waiting for his family to return.

Meanwhile, in Vitória da Conquista, a city in the interior of Bahia, Magda and the three boys lived with the building administrator's son, a pragmatic bank clerk who could only see the moon, the sun and the stars in the sky—as well as airliners at times. She was happier now. With Fogaça at her side, her fear had become panic—his friends from Petrópolis had come dangerously close.

Yes, she was an alien. Not from *Carinae*, but from Orion. Her name was Artemis—and her beautiful green eyes were multimedia instruments that photographed and filed every human detail. Then, in a mere blink, the data was zipped and sent in Lacteous-Oranian, via wireless internet, to her home planet.

With Magda's help, the Earth would soon belong to another civilization.

Monday

For the last five years and three months, Adália da Conceição, a refined confectioner, had used her Mondays to sculpt the glazed decorations, the final touch for her wonderful cakes. The texture was so soft that the cake would melt in your mouth, like a delicious cloud of sugar, mixed up with other ingredients whose recipe the secretive Adália would never reveal.

Adália ignored how she had become the most famous confectioner in Brazil. She didn't care about fame—all she cared for was her cakes. She invented a new, subtle detail every day, improving her recipes even more. She cared for the dough, which she mixed tirelessly, never using too much or too little force. She cared about the fillings, which could surprise everyone with a new, unexpected taste. She cared for the decorations. Ah, the decorations! For Adália, decorating a cake was like dressing it, and she demanded elegance. When she decorated her cakes, Adália was surrounded by an alchemist's aura, mindless of the world. She used and abused the common elements of sugar, yolk, lemon, and a rainbow of aniline—she had an excess of ideas which could confuse the mind. There wasn't a single person in the world who wouldn't feel touched by the sophistication, the rarity, the exquisite taste of Adália's cakes—all of them masterpieces.

Adália shrugged when she read her name in the most important social columns of Rio de Janeiro. She continued to wear her flip-flops and her usual clothes—flowered-print dresses, made with cheap cotton. Adália's vanity was limited to her impeccable apron, spotlessly white and to her head scarves, equally spotless—virginally white. She changed them quite often, for she believed perfect hygiene could be felt in the cakes, enhancing the taste. The cleanliness of the kitchen, the oven, the tables, the countless tools, also worried her. Not even the smallest spot could disturb the moment of creation. If by any chance she found the tiniest bit of dust or dirt in the wrong place or time, Adália would throw away the dough and start over. She didn't get angry and she didn't complain. Perfect cakes were her rapture and her fate.

Adália da Conceição's life started to change when those damned social column journalists caused such a commotion that her modest house in the Baixada Fluminense[6] was suddenly stormed with ladies surrounded by a cloud of French perfume, alighting from expensive cars, one more important than the other. They came with the most different requests: engagement cakes, wedding cakes, birthday cakes, anniversary cakes, even divorce cakes—and a funeral cake once. Adália loved making the funeral cake. She covered it with black roses, paying her tribute to the dead woman who wasn't quite dead yet— but would be soon, since she had been a moribund long enough, as the heartbroken daughter said when she ordered the cake to be served to the bereaved relatives, after the body

---

6 Low-income area near Rio de Janeiro, Brazil

was cremated and the ashes scattered.

Adália noticed they were really making sure the old lady wouldn't come back. Incinerating her wasn't enough. She created the decoration with an explosion of black; the recipe contained an abundance of prunes, ground chocolate, and tamarind juice— and a box of laxative pills. She'd decided to take revenge in the name of the dead woman—her heirs would spend a few days locked in the bathroom. And they did, especially the daughter, a glutton who'd dug too happily into her late freedom and Adália's cake, all too delicious. In spite of the diarrhea, nobody blamed the cake—it was too delicate and proper a treat for their sweet bereavement, and it couldn't possibly have been the cause of the disaster.

Before that episode awakened Adália's *murder instinct*, her never-desired fame had already pricked her bad side. In the afternoon when the most *soignée* matriarch of Rio de Janeiro's elite visited her to order, a year in advance, her granddaughter's wedding cake—a splendid affair, ten layers of sugar-frosted delicacy, decorated with a thousand flowers, and two live, white doves on top, which the bride and groom would free in honour of their own liberation—Adália's cake sank. It was the first and the only cake in Adália's life to ever sink in the oven.

Adália was desperate, and she hated the jasmine-smelling lady. She nearly refused the order—she hadn't done so for one reason—the big challenge of locking live birds in a sugar prison. That would require skills and she had no idea how she'd do it—but the lady had dared her, showing her the picture of an English princess's wedding cake, with two doped doves locked in the top. If the English had managed, so would she, and she wouldn't dope the birds she decided, while burying the useless cake—like a stillborn, in a hole she'd dug under the protective shadow of a backyard tree.

From that afternoon on, Adália da Conceição warned her distinct clientele that she wouldn't open the door to those wearing perfume, since the cakes were too sensitive—they lost their taste, their form and their elegance. She forbade that and felt relieved, in the hope that the ladies would rather die than leave the house smelling naturally. She was sadly mistaken. Adália's extreme measure was the topic of the first newspaper article about her—small as it was, only a six centimeters column, without a picture, but with a lot of fuss, praising the courage of the Baixada confectioner, who in defence of her art had dared to confront the Zona Sul[7] millionaires.

The day after the article was published, the street where Adália lived was invaded by a procession of cars. Rich ladies, deprived of all scent, came from every corner of Rio after those cakes, so delicate that the poor dough would lose its taste if stricken by aggressive fragrances. For hours on end, Adália faced the well-born, though classless crowd. They yelled, pushed, cursed—they wouldn't miss a chance of buying one of the famous Adália's cakes.

Annoyed, Adália—whose only desire in life was to make her cakes in peace, earning just enough money to have a good life in Baixada and improve her cooking skills even more—concluded that forbidding the perfumes hadn't been a well-thought out step. To keep the joy of her simple life, she only had one choice—asking a fortune for her cakes. The decorated cakes would reach stratospheric prices—then, she thought, *no one would disturb her.*

That proved to be another big mistake, and Adália paid

---

7 The South Zone is the richest and most fashionable residential area in Rio de Janeiro.

the price for it the rest of her days. Many people actually got into serious debt after finding out her cakes cost *an arm and a leg*—they had to have the honor of serving a sophisticated cake to their guests—even better, a designer cake. Poor Adália, her cakes became a sign of status, and whoever didn't have the pleasure of eating them had to suffer the humiliation of being excluded from the circles of power in Rio.

That was how Adália da Conceição's cooking taste changed her routine into a caramelized hell. One week, she was only Adália, the cake maker who loved her delicious creations, and the next, she had become the elegant Dona Adália, the sophisticated confectioner, surrounded by helpers and the owner of an industrial scale oven, a gift from the Mayor, who was thrilled by the money she was bringing to the municipality, as poor and needy as any in Baixada. Trying not to be rude, she accepted the monstrosity she didn't ask for or want. She loved her old-fashioned oven, and had it installed in the backyard.

Adália da Conceição took a long time to understand life's blow against her. In spite of her sudden fame, she kept her outfit of flowered dresses and flip-flops, the spotless aprons and the habit of preparing the cakes herself—from breaking the first egg to the final product. Her helpers, hired quickly by the Municipal Secretariat of Social Actions, took turns doing chores outside the kitchen—they swept the floor, did the laundry, went shopping for groceries, attended to the yard. One of them said he was an accountant and took charge of the bookkeeping. Adália was making a fortune, she didn't bother to check—so he, obviously, stole money from her.

To keep up with the deluge of orders, Adália da Conceição worked tirelessly until the day she fired all her helpers and declared herself on hiatus. She hated making cakes without pleasure. Her beloved cakes had taste, had a soul, had character and life.

"Orders, never more." That said, she locked herself at home and didn't deliver the engagement cake of the only daughter of the richest businessmen in São Paulo.[8] The press, who had adored her thus far, didn't spare the rude words that demoralized her. There wasn't a day when the headlines and columns didn't attack Adália—accusing her of being irresponsible, unable to honor a commitment. One particularly hard article, published in the Sunday edition, affirmed that Dona Adália had gone mad because of PMS or menopause. Adália, whose world was limited to her kitchen, was irritated with such nonsense. She didn't know a thing about sexism or feminism, but she did know how to make cakes and she loathed arrogant cakes, cakes of disrespect.

Fearful of Adália, who could cause a cataclysm in the economy of the area which had been restructured to tend to her needs and her distinct clientele—civil and religious authorities joined in their efforts to keep her working. Those were justifiable efforts. In a short time there arose in Adália's municipality and the surrounding areas a political crisis— unemployment rates skyrocketed, recession was happening again. Thousands of people who lived off her talent—of making the most delicious cakes in South America, perhaps in the world—were helpless.

Threatened and scared by the deficit in his budget, the Mayor decided to act and tried to pay a visit to Adália, who refused the honor. It was the Archbishop who interceded, trusting to the pious, kind, charitable Adália, of indisputable faith. Dressed in his purple robes and surrounded by acolytes—

---

8 The richest and most populated State in Brazil.

without bothering to announce his visit, the Archbishop entered the confectioner's home with the intimacy of the saints.

She couldn't possibly have been more accommodating. Welcoming the procession—the Bishop, monsignors, vicars, preceded by children dressed in angel costumes—Adália removed her flip-flops and put on shoes, in deference to the magnitude of the visitors. The conversation lasted much longer than the Archbishop imagined or wished—his bad mood was somehow improved by the slices of cake that Adália, in her state of grace, served him—although she refused to change her mind. She wouldn't take any more orders—she wouldn't make those exaggerated, vain mountains of sugar, ever again.

"Your Eminence must forgive me. But I make cakes as a philosophy. I'm concerned with their essence—not the vanilla's essence, naturally—although I don't despise it. I'm talking about integrity, distinction, honesty, those things that apply to cakes and humans. And that, Archbishop, does not exist in cakes made exclusively to humiliate others. I know Your Eminence understands me. Cakes are our brothers, just like any person. Appearance doesn't matter. What matters is sweetness, taste, dignity."

Before the eminent clergyman got irritated with his stray sheep, a runaway from the herd—a humble priest came up with a suggestion to save the day: If Adália agreed to go back to work, she would get full indulgence—meaning that her soul would be a *tabula rasa*, just like a newborn's, she'd go straight to heaven if she happened to die suddenly, with no previous warning: "You could be run over by a car, who knows?"

Touched, Adália surrendered. She promised the man of God she'd wear her apron again, "as a sign of gratitude to the Bishop and his indulgent forgiveness of all my mistakes and sins. Your Eminence is as good as the best cake."

The cake orders and the municipal pride were restored, and Adália went back to her personal hell, baking her futile cakes. Sadness invaded her. Adália da Conceição started to lose weight, to work without any motivation.

And then anger came. To take revenge on those who would deny her respite, Adália da Conceição started to spit in the dough, not just her spit but the drool of Uther, a filthy dog. The ingredients she used in her ire went beyond all reason. Out of spite she decided to add some extra elements to the recipes: bird crap; rainwater from potholes; moss from dirty stones; and once a month, her own menstrual blood. The more she invented revolting mixtures and used disgusting ingredients, the more people applauded her. The fact that nobody complained only added to her irritation. So, driven by pure evil, she decorated a child's birthday cake with ants—caramelized alive. It was a disturbing scene—the insects showed the horror of their death. Regardless of this the birthday boy's parents praised her, as well as the guests—they paid her endless compliments, blind to the deliberate cruelty.

Such insensitivity drove Dona Adália mad. Once again she closed her doors—it was her final decision. She'd only bake cakes, charging very low prices, for her neighbors and friends in the Baixada Fluminense. She explained:

"I don't care about money. The accountant was pocketing my profits, anyway. I just want to be happy making my sweet little cakes for those who understand them."

When the Mayor heard the news, he was furious. Before a recession ended his secret dream of becoming the State Governor, he decided to talk to Adália whether she wanted or not. *It's unbelievable. An ordinary woman, who doesn't even know how to dress, trying to ruin me. She'll see.*

Enraged, the Mayor quickly summoned his Secretaries, who were also desperate after Adália's second defection. Using a grave, studied tone of voice, the Supreme Chief of that shithole municipality declared that his main objective, from that day on, would be keeping Adália working, at least until Election Day.

"My substitute will have to deal with this madwoman, who talks to sugar as if it could understand her. I won't wait another second. I'm going to her house now. Those who love Baixada, follow me."

Bringing his whole Cabinet, including the Finance Secretary, a PhD renowned for creating fraudulent companies—the Mayor went straight to the humble house where Adália worked—received her orders and made her cakes. They arrived at a really bad time. Adália was concentrated on the last purposeless, futile cake she'd ever prepare in her life—or so she thought—a luxurious Torah for a jeweler's son's Bar Mitzvah. The father had donated powdered gold, so Adália could change it into a precious glaze, an exact reproduction of the religious text. Hebrew writing is difficult—Adália was innovating with the beauty of golden letters reflected in the miracle of powdered gold mixed with cat urine.

The authorities waited, one, two, several hours. It was almost evening when Dona Adália entered the living room, telling them that she had little time—only the necessary time for the Torah to dry. She had protected it from the heat, the humidity, the flies, the wind and the almost impossible cold of the air-conditioned room—the only luxury she had bought herself with the money that still kept coming in—the already wealthy accountant having given up stealing.

With her head spinning and thinking about measuring cups, Adália heard the blah-blah-blah about her inestimable value, and the value of her work. She heard, very vaguely, scientific explanations about ciphers and hierarchies. While those bores chatted, Adália da Conceição freed her mind and thought about other problems, for example, the following day's cake—*traditional, three tiers of different sizes, decorated with diamond accents. This jewel would be used in the 60th anniversary party of a mad couple—blessed by the glory of the Lord. Husband and wife knew the recipe for what common people call love, a sweetness which only lasts with respect. Only that way,* thought Adália—while the men kept on talking—*someone would reach the glory of giving themselves away without committing suicide.*

Finally, while the authorities continued to talk nonsense, Adália da Conceição had an idea—*in between the sugar drops, she'd put black flowers, as a preview of the bereavement reserved for one of the spouses. It wouldn't take long—whoever celebrates their Diamond Anniversary was married in kindergarten or had one foot in the grave,* she concluded, by changing her apron for the eighth time that day.

"We know all about that conversation. Besides the concrete fact that her production could only continue if it was very well organized..." Adália da Conceição didn't understand a thing—period. After a lot of discussion Dona Adália was extremely agitated and couldn't wait until the Mayor had disappeared—a marble statue in the city square. She finally accepted the idea of organizing a schedule—the initial step in successful management.

"Believe me, Dona Adália, if you organize your days, the pleasure of making cakes will make you happy again," said the Mayor, grinning from ear to ear.

Next came the doctor, a scientist devoted to time and management. In between graphs and organograms, he explained details that had saved and would save any and every company through a state of reorganization. Adália was over bored, so she pretended to understand everything, in the hopes she'd send the man home more quickly. She had already gotten the important facts—*instead of overworking, accumulating chores, she'd spread her tasks along the days of the week. Brilliant! How hadn't she thought of that before?*

She decided to give herself a new chance. Before giving up her profession, she'd try to adapt to the demands of the market place, which seriously lacked production on an industrial scale. That was how the Monday habit of sculpting fruits and flowers with sugar, making the decorations for the cakes, began.

Adália loved that day. She dismissed her helpers; collected thousands of beer bottle caps; and with the help of an icing-filled squirt, she created impossible things of stunning beauty. Time went by really fast—and Adália wouldn't notice. She could only understand that night was calling and she had to take some rest when there wasn't a single piece of furniture available to put the decorated caps on. Before going to bed, using a knife, she removed the decorations from the caps and put them in cans, with the lids closed so the art wouldn't melt.

Organization brought on boredom. And with boredom came the memories of happier days, when she baked her cakes contentedly, without the need to overwork. That was when a terrible idea started to form in her head—to poison a piece of decoration and mix it with the others, so she would never know which cake would bring someone's disgrace.

When Monday came, Adália da Conceição, desperate cake maker, needed to use the tranquilizers she kept in the drawer of her bedside table for sleepless nights—when her head felt like splitting and she ate the cakes which had mysteriously sunk. When such nights started to become more frequent, she exchanged her cheap dress for an equally cheap dress—but a little newer—and went to see a doctor.

The doctor diagnosed stress, and prescribed her sleeping pills, lots of them, so the cake maker could sleep in peace. The doctor wasn't wrong, you have to think big—*If the cake maker didn't sleep, the cake maker didn't work. If she stopped working, the municipality would stop, and so would the surrounding areas. The losses, the bankruptcies, the unpaid bills would arrive to the clinic and the doctor would drown in the ocean of debt. He owed his success to Dona Adália and couldn't even think about that—it was best to dope her,* he decided.

He kept her doped for years, time enough for Adália to build the reputation of the best confectioner in the world— and for him to amass a considerable fortune. Tranquilizers abounded, thanks to the good doctor. Without even examining her, he sent Adália the prescriptions she requested. What mattered most for the doctor was keeping Dona Adália working—with the right to a few hours of calm, chemically induced sleep.

And he managed to do just that. He'd never imagine that in her thirst for revenge, Adália would use the pills to poison the cakes—which was exactly what she did. She started by mixing a box of pills to the sugar necessary for the production of the decorations. In Adália's mind, there was no regret. Whoever worshipped her talents had condemned her to prison, and there was nothing more obvious than retribution.

Excited with the thrilling novelty of distributing death, Adália was reborn. She gained her weight back, she started smiling again and she worked happily—for she had found a way to give soul to her sophisticated, but meaningless cakes. Each order she received meant a cake would teach people *out there* that nobody has the right to bother anyone.

Poor Dona Adália. Once again, she had made the wrong choice—fate refused to help her in her pedagogical mission. Instead of causing some fateful death, the hidden tranquilizers never killed a single person. The worst they did was to induce the gluttons into a sweet, deep sleep—the already famous cakes became even more notorious. They were so delicious, people said, *they could calm you down*. After eating them, many people felt air headed and carefree; they slept for days—with a healthy expression and perfect breathing.

While she tried to manage her clients, desperate for their perfect cakes which could make people relax in pure joy—Dona Adália remembered the boring little man who was an expert in time management, and she understood her mistake—she hadn't calculated the correct dosage of sleeping pills. She needed to innovate in time engineering too—meaning, to incorporate a whole box of pills in a single bite, so as to avoid any chance of failure.

The following Monday she mixed 30 ground pills with a small quantity of sugar—a few drops of lemon juice and a subtle touch of aniline. With her death glaze—the *absolutely guaranteed* one—she sculpted a rose, in the most beautiful of shades—from the lightest pink to a soft orange, mauve, scarlet, deep red—a splendor of beauty. Whoever gave that rose a hungry bite would never suspect that they would be swallowing the final drama of their own lives. Very carefully, Dona Adália left her rose-trap to dry under the lamp on the bedside table. Then, as if nothing had happened, she continued her work, producing wonders.

Distracted, Dona Adália dedicated her entire day to making more delicacies—without noticing that the backyard of her modest house in Baixada Fluminense now sheltered a huge crowd that didn't stop growing. Her cakes had reached the status of miracle-makers, and the whole State of Rio came to see the confectioner—to touch her, interview her. The nearly *murdered*, surrounded by their relatives, hugged each other crying. Old and new clients, national and foreign members of the press, TV networks broadcasting live with shocking interviews, such as the lady whose mother had resuscitated, in spite of having been cremated and buried:

"The miracle happened because the family was honored with a cake by Dona Adália. It is true, something rare happened to us. How could we have imagined it was a message from mom, telling us she'd return?"

There were street vendors and onlookers—the crippled, asking for the grace of walking again and the blind, wanting to see again. Some people—men, obviously—wished not to fail at the *crucial time*—and there were those blessed by life, who'd always had so much and still wanted more. Every single person was sure that a cake by Dona Adália could heal all their pains.

Besides the Mayor and the Bishop—dressed in white robes, the color of resurrection—His Supreme Honor, the Governor himself had materialized in flesh and bone. He had come to that faraway place—a living hell of heat, mosquitoes, poverty—for a dual purpose. As well as collecting votes, he'd order a cake—an immense one, the biggest Dona Adália would ever dare to make. With the giant thing in the oven, he'd celebrate the nomination of his party to run for President of the Republic. The politician arrived with a well-rehearsed speech to the State of Rio de Janeiro, where a confectioner touched by the hand of God lived. She could bring back the dead and stop a gun from being fired. If Dona Adália's cakes had prevented a murder, what couldn't they do for the poor, the hungry of the

Northeast—for the millions of miserable people living in the streets—for Brazilian industry, for the production of crude oil, for a better distribution of income? He could see himself at the Palace, and raised his voice:

"Here, right before our eyes, a miracle happened. Let us all believe in the blessed cakes made by the blessed Dona Adália—patriotic cakes, saviors of the Nation. Cakes with a *fluminense*[9] soul, a soul I will spread from the North to the South of this country, ending the hunger of our suffering people..." And he would have continued the endless speech if Dona Adália, finishing her Monday chores, hadn't noticed the noise coming from the street. Curious, and eager to know what was happening, she didn't even change her apron, which unfortunately was stained with aniline of all colors. She'd barely opened the door when she saw flashes from the cameras, TV lights and a round of applause coming from the crowd, praising her blessed name. Utterly perplexed, she locked herself in the house again, swept by emotion:

"But what the hell is going on?"

Once again, the Archbishop saved the day. Through a closed window, the three of them confabulated—the Archbishop, Dona Adália and the humble priest, an expert in tricks who'd already convinced Adália to keep working with the promise of indulgence. She was inside the house, the other two were outside, their feet buried in mud because it had rained the day before—a disaster for the Archbishop, so mindful of his comfort.

Adália da Conceição felt the ground disappearing from under her feet when she heard the story from the Archbishop:

"Do you remember the cake you made for the wedding

---

9 Term referring to the people born in the State of Rio de Janeiro.

last Saturday?"

Adália da Conceição humbly answered:

"Yes your Eminence, a simple cake, only six layers. There was an airport with lots of sugar planes on the runway—if I'm not mistaken the groom is a pilot. But why all this commotion outside—why can't they ignore me?"

His Eminence explained, "Because you are a saint for your information. On Saturday, you prevented a tragedy—well, your cake did. The groom was living in sin—he was sleeping with someone else. The betrayed woman went to the reception, determined to kill the rival. Without the intervention of your super, sugar airport, the groom would now be a widower."

He narrated, with detail, the despair of the abandoned sinner, focusing on the attempts made by the guests to stop her from firing a gun at the bride and groom. He explained the angels' and saints' intercession, illuminated through the groom's sister's saving idea:

"Ok, if you want to kill her, kill her. My sister-in-law is an insufferable bore. But before you do that, don't miss the chance to try one of the famous Dona Adália's cakes. Where will you have another opportunity to taste a delicacy reserved for royalty? It cost an arm and a leg. Go, eat your cake in peace and then do what you have to do. I'll cover you."

"Wise words," the Archbishop continued. "They saved a sacrament famous for provoking tears, not an outrageous bloodshed—even though the Church has a tendency to cause useless bloodshed. But let's not change the subject. The thing is, the rejected woman ate the cake, calmed herself, lay down and slept. Your cake healed her wounds. You saved a life which will produce new lives, blessed by the sacred laws of matrimony. Come, my daughter, come and receive the glories the

Church has reserved for you. You are a humble woman, but the Son was humble, too. Open the door, Dona Adália, and welcome the people who only want to worship you."

Adália da Conceição heard the Archbishop talking with her eyes closed. Fat tears were streaming down her face, making her apron wet. She was nothing but useless. She couldn't even kill. On the contrary, she had managed to stop death, all because of the sleeping pills mixed with the glaze without any scientific method. It was pointless to try—everything she did went wrong.

Adália da Conceição had for years maintained her composure, controlled her emotions. She murmured that she'd get ready—so many people were waiting, she couldn't show up with a stained apron, unworthy of her cakes:

"If Your Eminence won't mind, I'll go and change my clothes. I'll open the door in a minute."

While the Archbishop, with an expression of eternal glory, told the crowd that the blessed Dona Adália would come soon, and that she'd just asked for some time to get ready—a natural thing for a lady, even a cake maker. Adália went to her bedroom, approached the bedside table, and with a decisive gesture swallowed the perfectly colored rose, already dry under the lamp.

TUESDAY

The successful engineer, Coriolando Bastos da Silveira e Souza was a cultured, travelled man, sophisticated and elegant—a very popular person among the elite of Rio, well married, father of three sons of exemplary behavior. And every Tuesday he crossed the shadows that split him in two. During the rest of the week, his personalities never greeted one another. On Tuesdays, the two celebrated with no regrets.

Thus far his path had been hard. Since his adolescence, Coriolando wandered the offices of every shrink in Rio de Janeiro—Freudian or Jungian, those who preferred Reich or a combination of the three, spiritualists, vanguard Masons etc. He had reached the age of 58 when he met a psychiatrist who followed the *pragmatic-Freudian theory*—a theory he had created and which only he himself practiced. Stretched on the couch, wearing shorts and sandals, Dr. Guilherme Paiva adopted his singular concepts learned during years of ambulatory practice in public hospitals. With poor, unhappy, underfed clients, always unwashed and badly dressed—people who were sick in body and soul—Dr. Guilherme had understood that theories are useless in the face of an emergency, and that life is too short to waste time discussing what is obvious. Despite not being orthodox, the doctrines learned with those who lived *in extremis* ended up making his Ipanema office famous. The doctor had no available time—bear in mind that he was able to solve any problem in only three sessions. Those who wanted mental masturbation, cursing their mothers, fathers, grandparents or a boring older sibling, could find another shrink. He used the direct approach—tit for tat. His existential punches, besides solving the problems of many good people, had also made him rich. And it was fair, everybody thought. Guilherme Paiva's methods were based on excellence.

The well-born of Rio had a lot of fun with the story of the rich, pretty lady who bore the weight of her days using anti-depressants, crying in her penthouse, looking at the sea. After one single session, she left her husband, the pills and Vieira Souto Avenue. She became *alternative*. She wore simple clothes and flip-flops, ate alfalfa and cereal and played the bagpipe in the organic garden of her small farm in Vargem Grande, a refuge where the ex-millionaire had a love nest with the ex-driver of her ex-brand new Jaguar. She had lost the car in the divorce, but did not care. She was poorer, but better loved and happier.

After waiting six months for a slot in the shrink's schedule, Coriolando showed up at the office, well-groomed and neatly brushed, with the triumphant attitude of a successful engineer. Doctor Guilherme Paiva just looked at him once and solved the riddle. Efficient and practical, he went straight to the point that had cost fortunes, irrecoverable years and permanent anguish to poor Coriolando.

"Coriolando, my friend, your problem isn't sexual; it is philosophical. You are a faggot, but you refuse the label.

What's the point? You've gone through the most difficult part; you did it and liked it. By the way, you keep doing it and enjoying it. So why the anguish? Why the fear of coming out of the closet? Stop being a sissy, man. You are a faggot, end of story. People who worry too much about names—people who have problems with the label but never with the act, really piss me off. You don't say no to a man on your back, but reject the aggressive word, in horror. Look, if the word faggot bothers you, call yourself something else. Everything in life is so simple, for God's sake, what a bunch of complicated people!"

Coriolando was offended with the affront of that speech. He thought about punching the doctor: *What a little son of a bitch of a doctor; he just opened up my wound.* Vexed, he decided to face the problem:

"I am sorry to inform you, doctor, but I am not gay, I am bisexual. I like women too, and to be honest, I'm quite good in the sack. I've never heard complaints."

The doctor scratched his head, looking straight at Coriolando:

"Listen, my friend, and try to understand something: bisexuals are gay. This thing of bisexuality is a modern idiom and it only complicates things. Never mind, though; it is your body, and nobody has anything to do with the story. Just take care of yourself and live your pleasure without guilt. What an old-fashioned attitude! Everyone wants to be macho in Brazil! If you like doing it, do it, what is the problem? Come on, man, don't make things difficult."

Defeated, Coriolando lowered his head. *Damn doctor!* He preferred the others, to whom he paid fortunes, just to feed his doubts:

"You are competent, but you'd better remember: I am not gay. Gays only like men, and I like men and women."

"Congratulations on your good taste. Women, even when they're bad, are wonderful. I prefer women, personally. But when you like them, and only them—do you understand?—*This* is *not* being gay. If you sleep with men and women, whether you like it or not, you *are* gay. Your case is easy, Coriolando. You just need to accept yourself and stop wallowing in remorse. If it's any consolation, I have seen worse dramas. Do you want an example? A super macho forty-something, tortured by doubt about homosexuality. We had proof when I told him to test things in practice. The poor man vomited for a week—made death threats, felt insulted. Afterwards he kissed my hands, happy with the discovery of his full maleness—already scarred. But I only had one choice—if I hadn't chosen shock treatment, he would have spent a century without any resolution. You're different. I just needed to hear you to know. What could be better, Coriolando? You are a ready-made faggot, a finished work. All will be well when you swallow the word that bothers you so much. It will hurt a little, but this whining anguish that torments your days will disappear in a second.

The family was worried. Coriolando's case seemed to be serious. The treatment with Dr. Guilherme Paiva lasted for exactly seven sessions, two times the normal length.

Actually, Coriolando was cured in the first session. He left with the certainty that he had definitely been born a faggot, a certainty that hurt, but that also allowed him to live with tranquility. He could even enjoy having a partner, now—if he met one. His reputation as a married-with-children engineer, however, scared any potential partners away. *The fact—* thought Coriolando, in his first morning of freedom—*was that Dr. Guilherme Paiva deserved his fame. Only one hour had been enough for him to calm me down. He could convince me that just because I like doing it with men, doesn't mean I will offend others.*

The next six sessions were dedicated to solve Coriolando's practical problems—after all, coming out of the closet in middle age could mean war. As Dr. Guilherme had said:

"You have to act carefully, very carefully. You started out wrong. Gays must not get married. Whoever thinks they're going to be able to maintain appearances always ends up in trouble. Look at your case. At this point, it is impossible to come clean. There's a wife, children, clients, it's too complicated. So, let's be practical."

Thanks to Dr. Guilherme Paiva's objectivity, millions of light years ahead from reigning psychiatric practices, Coriolando Bastos da Silveira e Souza was able to balance the gay and the conservative sides of his personality—something definitely crazy. Trying to deal with two unsuspected lives—the macho's routine and the gay's happiness—the doctor was exasperated. He confessed that he could not understand how Coriolando would satisfy his two egos without going totally nuts:

"Congratulations, Coriolando, you are the most complex psychopath I have ever encountered in my career. To survive almost 60 years walking a razor's edge is not for everyone, but my darling, it's time to be free. I will help your gay side to emerge completely, without damaging your reputation of a traditional, family and societal pillar."

Doctor and patient discussed what was virtually impossible, how Coriolando would maintain the *status quo* without giving up living in peace with his gay side—something difficult, but solvable. Dr. Guilherme Paiva deserved a Nobel Prize. He had analyzed in detail a course to protect his client from the cruelty of others:

"First of all, keep your macho attitude. If you really like women, find yourself a lover, to keep appearances. Be careful! Don't forget the condoms and don't come back here horrified after killing someone. HIV does not forgive, and you are responsible for whatever happens."

After a lot of discussion, the strategies were elaborated and the doctor decided that Coriolando could accept his feminine side without guilt, one day a week—always away from Rio.

"Only one day?" He complained.

"Don't be a bore, man. You came to me with your head full of doubts, and now you tell me one day is not enough? Is this a joke? One day a week, and thank God for that. But don't forget: If I hear that you have screwed things up in Rio de Janeiro, I will call a journalist who owes me a few favors and tell her you are a Catholic pedophile. You have to convince yourself that once a week is great for your age. What are you whining about?"

Coriolando still did not like it. Tuesdays were the beginning of the week, just when the company was full of problems with the builders. That was also the day when the financial market set the atmosphere for the week; his wife said the rosary with her friends; and he went home—after the prayers, of course—to play the role of impeccable host. One of his sons had developed the habit of defeating him in chess.

"Can't it be another day?"

"Coriolando, please. Don't bother me. I chose Tuesdays because it's the day of the gay parties during Carnival. Are you going to keep whining?"

That was an irrefutable argument. On that exact moment, Coriolando made peace with himself. Thanks to the wisdom, the experience, the intelligence, the subtlety and the rudeness of Dr. Guilherme Paiva, Coriolando Bastos da Silveira e Souza became a happy Tuesday faggot—the other six days were dedicated to his role as *pater familias*. Dr. Guilherme, the hero, had loosened the rope that had been strangling him, suffocating him slowly.

He set off towards the future with his head full of dreams. Walking the streets of Ipanema, he noticed the beauty of the day. It had been years since he had last noticed the clarity of Rio: the air seemed to sparkle. He drove to the office whistling and spent the whole day happy. The employees saw—and talked about—the sudden change of mood of their temperamental boss. Coriolando laughed, talked and did not shout at the secretary. His partner, university classmate and longtime friend, decided to confront him:

"I think you've been acting strange. Has something happened?"

"You've got the wrong impression. I feel great. The company is going wonderfully, there's a grandchild on the way, I've found a girl, man, and she's a hottie. And to make things even better, I've just found out that my name has been approved by the strictest Brazilian association of cigar tasters. Don't you think I should be happy?"

"Cigars? You've never smoked cigars!"

"My friend, I've smoked cigars since I was a teenager. If you didn't know about that, what can I do? The thing is, from this week on I'll be going every Tuesday to the Association meetings in São Paulo, and you will take care of the office alone. My dear friend, I am a happy man.

The scene was repeated at the dinner table, that same evening. During the afternoon, Coriolando had called his wife and asked her to call the children. He had an important announcement to make.

"Prepare a special menu and put the champagne on ice."

He did not say much else, despite his wife's insistence. He just told her that it was good news, so good that she received roses and a passionate note. A happy soul always overflows; it wants to share the joy—dear God, being gay is such fun!

Nothing in this life is easy, however. Despite Coriolando's efforts to maintain a happy environment, the dinner when he told his family—that after years of trying he had finally managed to get his name approved by the Brazilian Association of Cigar Tasters, a select group which only accepted true experts—was a giant failure. After telling them that from next week on, he would be travelling to São Paulo every week, Coriolando raised his glass:

"To success and to cigars!"

Astonished, the whole clan raised their glasses, but the youngest son could not avoid asking:

"Dad, what madness is this? You don't smoke, you choke with the smell, and now you've become an expert in cigars overnight?"

When the wife saw the bait she was waiting for thrown on the table, she left the room. Composed and self-controlled, after all, ladies never lose their poise, she stopped at the threshold, holding back the tears:

"If there's another woman, save me the embarrassment of hearing it from a stranger."

Chaos ensued. Sons and daughters-in-law gave their support to the likely betrayed woman; Coriolando got upset and started to give a speech—he had been a workaholic his whole life, working as a slave to give comfort to his family, and when he indulged himself in a little pleasure, smoking a little cigar in São Paulo, there was anarchy.

"There's no other woman, I love my wife. I love my children too; I'm in seventh heaven with my unborn grandchild. Hell, can't I smoke a little cigar in peace?"

The pregnant daughter-in-law was touched:

"Dr. Coriolando, you are cute, but can't you smoke in Rio? Why do you have to travel so far? If it were Cuba, with Fidel Castro, we could understand. But a mason cigar association based in São Paulo? I don't know, this sounds really weird—my poor mother-in-law."

The poor mother-in-law, in tears and surrounded by the children, mourned the womanizing ways of her husband, unable to resist a short skirt. Swallowing her sobs, she swore that the crazy story could only be the excuse for an affair:

"Another whore, to add to the dozens your father has had."

The drama lasted enough to make Coriolando agree that he would bring home the Association document the following day—a paper proving the inclusion of his name in the group and confirming the weekly meetings every Tuesday, which had been produced by Dr. Guilherme's secretary after a careful Internet search for names of first-class cigars. Seeing the evidence, wife and children were pacified and Coriolando could plan his first trip to São Paulo, a routine he followed religiously until the day of his death, a few years later. He left Rio Monday evening, catching the last available flight, and returned on Tuesday, also on the last flight.

The beginning of the weekly holiday of his maleness was complicated. On the plane, Coriolando found himself overwhelmed by a mixture of feelings: fear, shame, desire, shyness, a sudden urge to go back home. He did not know the gay ghettos or the popular places among his comrades. In the hotel room, he spread cigar ashes on his clothes—Dr.

Guilherme's advice so the family would believe he had spent 24 hours smoking—and thought of himself as a fool.

But when the will is so strong, there is no obstacle. During his second trip, Coriolando lived his first adventure. On the tenth, he was part of the gang. He had never felt so happy—a happiness that he extended to his family, his office, his friends. Coriolando changed. His wife and sons were delighted with this new man who gave affection freely. His employees made extra efforts in their daily chores; Dr. Coriolando was generous with pay raises. Either you are lucky, or you are not—and Coriolando was. He gave meaning to his friends, who envied his countless achievements; when his grandson was born he was named after him. The proud grandfather celebrated the baptism with a Hollywood-like party, walking around happily with the little boy on his lap, but hiding from the photographers. He shivered at the thought that someone in São Paulo, seeing him in the newspaper, would discover his secret.

The Association of Cigar Tasters, more orthodox than a fundamentalist religion, did not stop meeting even during Carnival. In his first Gala Gay ball, Coriolando wore a Spiderman costume, covered from head to toe, despite the heat—he loved the novelty of having so much fun in the city that sheltered his male personality, fooling Dr. Guilherme in the process. After the tenth shot of whisky, spacing out already, Coriolando started to believe that he would be able to control a third personality. So he incorporated Spiderman. He climbed walls, threw himself from the stairs, hung himself on the curtains, jumped from one balcony to another, and finally fell on top of a tourist's head, injuring the poor man. Trying to avoid further trouble, the security guards—handsome, blonde, tall, strong, Jesus, *what* were those men?—grabbed him and threw him out. Not even that fazed Coriolando. Torn, hurt and drunk, he waved goodbye and blew kisses to the audience. It was glorious.

Thanks to Dr. Guilherme Paiva's simple logic, Coriolando found himself. He had absolutely everything—in one city, respectability, money, success, family; in the other, no limits—access to all sorts of pleasure, the opportunity to explore all emotional frontiers. Coriolando did not take too long to notice that he had started to smoke cigars, with a five decade delay—wasted time, an unforgivable foolishness.

Six years after the first Tuesday in São Paulo, and after sleeping with hundreds of friends, Coriolando met the man he fell in love with; true passion and love, of the sort that invades the soul with an incontrollable urge to drown in tenderness, protect the partner, spoil him, give him all attention.

Doubt started to bother Coriolando again. He felt weird with his family—the grandchildren were four, now. When he felt guilty, he showered his wife with presents. He took her on their thirtieth trip to Europe, bought her all imaginable gifts—including a fur coat which cost over 20 thousand dollars, without complaints, although he could not imagine what that would serve for in the Rio de Janeiro summer. He fulfilled the role of dedicated husband efficiently, never forgetting to call São Paulo everyday when no one was watching.

The more he fell in love, the more unpredictable he became. The tolerant grandfather who used to roll on the floor with the children became suddenly irritated. He locked himself in the bedroom, counting every second until next Tuesday. He thought about killing and dying, he hated himself and the world. He considered selling his share in the company. He would have done that, if his sons, also engineers, had not replaced him on the board of directors. His business partner and friend received the brothers in his office, making a nearly accurate diagnosis:

"Well, boys. Coriolando has changed a lot since he became a member of the cigar association. Do you think he's drinking that Santo Daime tea? I don't know, the man seems to be crazy."

He did not only seem to be crazy, Coriolando felt he was really losing his mind. Suffering with the absence of the distant partner, he went to sleep and woke up thinking of his family. Opposite feelings suffocated him. He spent the whole week waiting for Tuesday, and when it came, his heart sank with the fear of never coming back, losing his wife and sons, seeing his macho reputation go down the drain.

It was too much pain for just one man. Coriolando thought about seeing Dr. Guilherme, a measure he finally took when he caught himself thinking about the possibility of coming out of the closet and publicly admitting his passion for Alberto P. Coimbra, an engineer like him, in his fifties, bachelor, member of the Association—and his soulmate.

In a panic, Coriolando set an appointment. To justify the urgency, he said it was a serious case, he was at the brink of committing suicide, and managed to jump the waiting line. Sweating, scared, he sat before his doctor and threw up the entire drama. Guilherme Paiva decided to play the fool:

"Oh, you are not bisexual? What's new?"

"I am bisexual, I have a lover, I actually need to see her. But this is not what I came here to talk about..."

Aiming straight at the target, the doctor interrupted him:

"Ok, I know. You have fallen in love. Listen, Coriolando, I told you the first time you came here: you are gay. Your current problem is simple: either you come out of the closet or you don't. I would not. If you were 20 years old, I would tell you to do it. But in your sixties, I think it is dangerous. Just think about it: a heart attack, a stroke, cancer, all the shit that can kill you is just around the corner, waiting for you. Is your lover going to look after you with the same affection your wife would? You have been married to her for forty years. What if you get sick? Can your boyfriend make chicken soup like she can? I seriously doubt it. Only if he is a chef! Normal men buy ready-made soup and all of those taste the same. Damn it, Coriolando, you were doing so well! Why did you get into this mess? You know, I always get surprised with the human ability to complicate things. Not even doctors can put a mad head back on the shoulders."

Willing to try to live with Alberto day and night, Coriolando told his family that he would travel to Cuba with the Association for a week, from Tuesday to Tuesday:

"We will try the new cigars Fidel is bringing into the market."

"Oh, go to hell, who needs to understand that much about cigars?"

Coriolando pretended not to have heard his son's comment. Rudeness had no place in his well-brought up family; they were well-behaved people, incapable of saying vulgar words. Besides, if the young man was suspicious, better for him. He would suffer less when the nuclear bomb his father was carrying in his pocket went off.

In two days, Coriolando was leaving for Bahia with Alberto P. Coimbra. Days of dream and glory. Coriolando could not stop thinking of his wife, a poor doomed woman who had wasted her life. With her, Coriolando had never known the delight, the blind and eternal madness of total surrender; perfect, dreamlike days which seemed to last just seconds. On the flight back, the lover disembarked in São Paulo. Coriolando said goodbye promising eternal love:

"I'll ask for the divorce tonight. I'll call you tomorrow morning and then I'll move here."

Too much stress, too much fear, too much life, too much love. Coriolando Bastos da Silveira e Souza died on Tuesday night, the same day he came back from the trip to Bahia; a sudden and fatal heart attack which took the family by surprise. The high society of Rio, shocked and saddened with the loss of that singular man, went to his funeral. One of the attendants was a representative of the Brazilian Association of Cigar Tasters, Dr. Alberto P. Coimbra, who said he had been waiting for a phone call from his friend to talk about the score given to a cigar blend they had tasted in Havana. Well-dressed and well-spoken, he approached the widow to offer his condolences:

"I called him and learned of the terrible news. I bring you my condolences, as well as the Association's. I am truly shocked."

And he was. He laid a bouquet of blood-red roses on the deceased's chest. He cried when the casket was closed. He followed the procession, supporting the son who had made the derogatory comment about his father. If Alberto P. Coimbra had not reacted quickly, the desperate man would have thrown himself into the grave.

The kind attitude of the man delighted Coriolando's family and friends, who started to see with different eyes the Association they believed had killed him. The feelings were returned, since Alberto P. Coimbra, trying to hold on to the man he had loved, asked permission to visit the family. He went to Coriolando's office and offered his services to his business partner, if the company needed him:

"I'm an engineer. I'll be honored if I can pay a tribute to my friend, talking the place of his sons during these days of mourning."

He was really charming. So charming that they let him stay. Alberto took care of the inventory, without making a single mistake. While Coriolando's sons cried, he rolled up his sleeves and worked in the company with great effectiveness. He never forced his hand. He helped discreetly, talking only when necessary, and avoided smoking cigars—and similarly shaped things. One day, questioned about the Association, he changed the subject elegantly:

"I'd rather not talk about it. It reminds me of my friend, it makes me sad."

He eventually married the widow. He took over half of the firm and soon detected some administrative slips. He corrected them and doubled the company's profits. Less than a year later, he bought his partner's share. He won his stepsons over, and was a fantastic grandfather, even more affectionate than Coriolando. Alone with his thoughts, however, he was astonished with fate, which could invent maneuvers to surprise God Himself—how could he, a declared homosexual, have got into that situation? He was not only married, but rich and happy, thanks to Coriolando.

Routine, however, is merciless. When daily life had no novelty anymore, Alberto's mind, body and soul became restless, and then came the memories of the Brazilian Association of Cigar Tasters. Shocked, for he had thought he would never leave the comfortable life of a millionaire in Rio, the expert hid his emotions, but told his wife he had been feeling a bit depressed:

"I haven't slept well lately."

She immediately suggested that he set an appointment

with Dr. Guilherme Paiva:
    "He's a great doctor, he cured Coriolando…"

WEDNESDAY

Few families could say they had such a devoted father. To raise his six children with all the luxuries they deserved—private schools, English classes, ballet for one daughter, gym for another, judo, football, dentists, doctors, new clothes and trips to Disneyworld—Waldemar Lopes Piraí de Souza, called Piraí by his friends and Piraí-my-love by his beloved wife, worked like a madman from sunrise to sunset. He worked so hard he only came home on Wednesday afternoons. On Thursdays, before noon, he said goodbye to his family and hit the road again.

He was a travelling salesman and worked as representative for a pharmaceutical company, one of the best in the field of natural products. Whoever needed to cleanse their intestines with the precision of a Swiss clock, could definitely use his teas, capsules and infusions; Piraí swore it all worked, with the sureness of a plant expert who seemed to have the magical knowledge of old Indian healers.

Sexual impotence? Digestion problems? Kidney stones? Verminosis? Family and friends waited eagerly for his visits on Wednesdays; he gave free consultations and distributed free samples of phyto-therapeutic drugs. Piraí never noticed, but his wisdom triggered the creation of a community of fanatical followers of holistic medicine in Honório Gurgel, a suburb of Rio de Janeiro. "Sane mind, sane body," repeated the salesman. That was why, before writing any prescription, he liked to hear the patients' complaints.

There was no living soul in the neighborhood who did not love such tenderness and care. Piraí was well-known for the gentle affection he dedicated to his brothers and sisters. Always smiling and good-humored, he helped anyone, regardless of belief or race. He understood people's dramas, consoled the sorrows, and gave friendly advice. When the case was serious, and the use of antibiotics or surgery was necessary, he referred the patient to the nearest hospital; but for small maladies, he used his powers of shaman—and he was good at it. Only on Wednesdays, though.

Thanks to a meticulous time management, Piraí helped the sick without neglecting his children. He picked them up at school, analyzed their report cards, talked to them, laughed with them, told them stories; Wednesdays were like a party at the family home. Dona Maria Augusta, the wife—a very, very, very lucky woman, as she always repeated, overflowing with emotion—woke up every Wednesday with her heart in her throat. After the patients left and the children were in bed, Piraí turned into Piraí-my-love, a skillful lover, until sunrise. Every week, he made up for the days of absence and gave her something to remember him by during the lonely, empty days.

While Piraí was travelling, Dona Maria Augusta was always sighing around the house, remembering every moment spent with him the previous Wednesday and planning the next. Every Wednesday brought her husband, a perfect companion, a wonderful friend and lover. They made a happy couple, and the only flaw in the relationship was the fact that Piraí always disappeared for the rest of the week.

To be fair, Piraí was never an absent father. He called the children every day, in the morning, in the afternoon and at night. Always a reserved man, he felt embarrassed to share his life with colleagues— other salesmen who stayed in cheap hotels to save money, just like him. After all, the money he earned was for his family.

On the phone, with a mysterious voice, Piraí followed the birth and the growth of his children, all made on a Wednesday night. On the phone, he chose their names: Maria de Fátima, Paulo José, Maria da Conceição, Pedro Tiago, João Lucas and Jesus César. The last one was baptized against the will of Dona Maria Augusta, who was a History teacher and thought it was wrong to mix two different cultures, Christian and pagan, in the same name. Piraí, however, insisted and convinced her. The youngest child became a walking religious syncretism, although nobody noticed. Only the mother, who had invented the nickname Jecé, a combination of the first syllables of Jesus and César, in an attempt to forget the philosophical slip of her husband, who united the executor and the victim in the same birth certificate.

"Poor Jecé. Piraí must have been selling diarrhea medicine when he chose that name."

The name Jesus César caused one of the rare fights between the couple, who had the perfect marriage. They loved each other madly and adored their children. While Piraí travelled the entire Brazilian territory selling drugs, Dona Maria Augusta taught History at the local school and looked after the children, waiting for Wednesdays.

She deserved all the credit; despite Piraí's phone calls,

she had the job of raising the six children alone. Illnesses, falls, school fights, choosing new schools, the difficult teenage years—all bombs blew up in her hands. Depending on the matter, she would wait and talk about the subject with her husband. When the case was too serious, she used the phone—when he called, of course. Piraí travelled so often that there was no way he could give his family an emergency telephone number. But even with the one-sided communication, Dona Maria Augusta trusted him blindly and always supported him. He received the news of rewards and punishments, always by phone.

Ah, love. Because she loved the volatile Piraí with all her body and soul, Dona Maria Augusta could stand living alone, never going anywhere, unless she had the company of one of the children. It was worth it. If life did not allow them to love their children together, she found consolation thinking about the day when the old couple would love every grandchild.

"Your father is made of gold," she used to say to herself and to the kids, when things got heated up during endless fights, or when her longing seemed to explode in tears.

Children and accidents, however, make an inseparable pair. One fine day, Maria da Conceição, a well-behaved and obedient girl, exaggerated in her playfulness and fell off a mango tree. The neighbors helped, returning Piraí's affection and attention. In a matter of minutes, the girl arrived to the hospital, followed by her mother and a crowd of friends; hundreds of people surrounding Dona Maria Augusta, bathed in tears, worried about her daughter who could be at the brink of death. She never prayed so hard Piraí would call: the family's maid had stayed home, with the task of telling her boss when he called.

After a few hours, the maid called Dona Maria Augusta

to give her Piraí's message. He could not come; he would close an important deal in the interior of Goiás within the next days. Besides, who would pay for his ticket? He had to worry with the hospital bills. Saddened, the messenger finished her task: "Mr. Piraí told you to find support in your relatives, friends and neighbors. He said he trusts you to make the right decisions and all will be well. Next Wednesday he will come to see Conceição.

Astonished with the fact that Piraí had refused to come see his own daughter—her husband, a man so devoted to others—Dona Maria Augusta was suspicious; there was something wrong. She had been so enchanted with the blessed Wednesdays, with Piraí's love, with the endless job of raising six children, that she had never noticed one strange detail: she had never met her mother-in-law. Whether she was boring, nice, friendly or nosey, it did not matter, she was the children's grandmother. Where would she be? What about brothers and sisters-in-law? And nephews and nieces? Did her husband really have a family? Families should always be together, to share the good and the bad things—besides fighting, of course.

Anyway, fights did not matter at that tragic moment. What mattered was counting upon the strength of blood, always loyal when threatened. Dona Maria Augusta's clan had materialized in seconds. Without the help of her uncle, friend of a friend of a cousin of the neurosurgeon, Maria da Conceição would not have received immediate assistance. They called the specialist, who came out of good will, thanks to the family's connections; after all, a first-class patient, niece of a friend of a friend of his cousin, should not wait for medical care.

The diagnosis was simple; it was just a concussion, nothing very serious. The doctor gave the news cheerfully to the mother:

"You don't need to worry. Just a little rest will take care of this."

The following week, Piraí found Conceição at home, free from any danger. Sitting beside the little girl, Dona Maria Augusta did not smile. She actually received her husband as if she wanted to throw stones at him.

"Is this the behavior of a father? Conceição was unconscious, her body was all purple from the fall, she was nearly in a coma, and you were wandering around. There is a limit to everything. You abused your luck, abused Conceição and abused me! Paying the hospital bills? What hospital bills? It's a public hospital! Conceição is well thanks to my brother, who knows everybody. If he hadn't interfered, she would have died on a stretcher in the corridor, while her father was selling medicinal plants so the people in Goiás would be able to crap. Oh, please. We need to talk, Piraí. Fathers do not stay away when a child suffers an accident. This is all very weird; you are hiding something from me. Where is your family? Why doesn't this laboratory have an office? A place I can call and leave messages? Who are you, Piraí?"

Piraí reacted ferociously to the last insinuation, scaring his wife. With an altered tone of voice, louder than usual, he explained he was only Waldemar Lopes Piraí de Souza, an abandoned child, raised in an orphanage, submitted to sadness and humiliation. He had told her almost everything before they got married and build a home that deserved the name:

"Now, I am a father who works day and night, without rest, to give our children what life denied me. Please, forget about this subject, these are torturing memories."

Touched and full of remorse for having opened the

wound that she actually knew—although the orphanage was news, and she could have sworn by the Bible that the previous version of the story included an alcoholic mother—Dona Maria Augusta apologized and suggested that her husband take some vacation time to stay home for a little longer. Piraí changed the subject:

"Let me see Conceição."

And that was how the soap opera of Piraí's vacations, always postponed, began. The discussion lasted for years, because the couple only met on Wednesday to talk about the plans. Maria da Conceição climbed the mango tree again a few times, but soon she gave up the botanical adventures: she started to date a bank clerk and eventually got married. Maria de Fátima also got married, and gave birth to three healthy boys. Conceição became a widow, due to a stray bullet that hit the bank clerk's head. Paulo José graduated in Astronomy and moved to California to study for his master's degree. Pedro Tiago became a doctor. João Lucas, the disaster—there's always one in every family —decided to become a painter of the abstract neo-avant-garde style. There was only Jecé at home, who was in high school. But Dona Maria Augusta still wanted Piraí to take vacations.

"You need to teach your grandchildren that male human beings just don't come and go as they please."

Piraí shot back, trying to get the support of his children:

"Maria de Fátima, tell your mother what a good father I am."

"You are great, daddy. But I want a father who's at home every day for my children. That's why I married Geraldo, a humble civil servant, who comes home every night."

Unshaken by the victorious expression on his wife's face with the young woman's answer, Piraí explained that people who had children needed money:

"My fate is to work. I will take vacations when Jecé gets married and follows his own path. Ah, there's Conceição, too: young, widowed and helpless.

Conceição, the widow, was dating again and Jecé had just turned sixteen. Maria Augusta insisted:

"My God, why don't you just take these damn vacations? I'm going mad!"

The fight would have continued *ad aeternum* if Piraí hadn't showed up the next Wednesday with salvation in hands. The humiliated wife felt she had lost the fight:

"Here. You wanted vacations, right? Here are the tickets. You are going to Disneyworld with Conceição and Jecé. The tour leaves in two weeks."

The mother did not share the excitement of the children with the trip abroad. She went against her will, and found everything extremely boring. The trip was only worth it because of Jecé's sudden interest in the perfect functioning of the parks—swimming alligators, elephants that raised their trunks at a precise moment, scaring the tourists. Instead of following the norm, getting excited with the movie characters and the rides and taking pictures with Mickey, Jecé bothered the poor Americans in charge of the park, insisting in visiting the computer room. He did not get to. He got back to Brazil with the sure decision of discovering each and every mystery related to computers. That was when hell said hello to the unfortunate Piraí.

The first computer was a Christmas gift. Faithful to his principles of giving everything to his children, stimulating their talents, Piraí made a loan and bought his son a super machine, as well as state-of-the-art accessories. If there had been more to buy, he would have bought it. He was beaming with pride with Jecé's knowledge about the new science that conquered the world with a click of a mouse.

Jecé followed the steps of any rookie computer whiz: he exchanged messages, had long conversations in chat rooms, visited dating sites and did research for his school assignments. Little by little, his talents became more sophisticated. He devoured computer books and surfed the Internet during his free time, forgetting all else. As a result, he started to learn more, more, and more. He became the star of modernity in Honório Gurgel, and earned his own money assembling and fixing computers, building websites, selling pirate recordings of CDs and illegally hacking other people's machines. He was a success. And this success became a complication when Jecé cheerfully announced during a Wednesday dinner that Piraí would never have to travel to sell his products again:

"Dad, I have a surprise for you. Now, anyone who wants your products will just have to access our website. It has endless information, incredible links, a shopping cart, a personalized email account, a virtual ombudsman. It's great! Your job has finally become modern, and now you have joined e-commerce. We will get rich! Using technology, we will double your profits and you won't even have to leave home. I've been thinking we could set up our own natural products representation company, fitopirai.com. Wouldn't that be awesome?"

Dona Maria Augusta did not understand half of the words Jecé had said, but she noticed that her boy had created something miraculous so his father could leave the travelling life, wandering round and round with no chance of rest. She was so excited with the idea coming from the brilliant mind of her son—his name wasn't Jecé by chance; he had united the bits & bytes of the future to the herbs and infusions of millenary tradition—that she did not notice the sudden paleness on her husband's face. Sitting at the head of the table, Piraí nearly choked with the chicken bone he was peacefully sucking. He had not understood half of Jecé's speech either, but he could sense the threat. His lack of understanding could only be a miracle of God, our Holy Lord, who had come from heaven in time to save him from that mess:

"Son, I didn't understand anything. Could you please repeat everything using normal words?"

With the bored air of the unrecognized genius, Jecé explained patiently what a website was and how it was used; the thousand ways the Internet could be used for sales; that they could sell Piraí's teas and plants to China, if they so desired; and that there was a real possibility that the Piraí family could become the owner of a virtual pharmaceutical company.

"If we don't do this, someone else will. The Internet has no limits. There is a space for us and we should take it, and the sooner, the better."

All those years of lies had taught Piraí to keep appearances. With his heart in his throat, really believing Jecé's proposal—damn stupid life, when a chance comes, I cannot take it—Piraí left the table. Calmly putting the chair back into place, he looked into his son's eyes:

"It's impossible, Jecé. People who buy medicines need to trust the seller, see them face to face. Forget this crazy idea, it will never work."

It is unnecessary to talk about Jecé's insistence and the support he got from his sibling Paulo José—who called from California and sent hundreds of emails begging his father not to hesitate in entering the New Era—and his brothers-in-law, since Conceição had remarried. Dona Maria Augusta, realizing that the discussion about Piraí's vacation had taken a different direction, thought about committing suicide. The years came and went, and the family was discussing the reasons for the old-fashioned dad's reluctance to accept the advantages of fitopirai.com.

When, as a last resort, the children used the argument of old age coming and the anguish of their mother, who felt more and more alone, Piraí finished the discussion solemnly with a stupid argument:

"I will always work with the strength of my hands. You want to rob me of my dignity, my male pride."

He did not even wait for an answer. He left to sell his drugs just like the old days—old days that had really gone, overcome by science which changed life into a screen.

So the boys got married, and each one chose his own path, making his own way in the world which spun faster, running out of space. The father had lost the enchantment of those times when he knew more than them. Wednesdays were bitter now. The Piraí family, bored and upset, seemed to drag on the stubborn patriarch.

Time went by slowly, with no excitement or joy. Every Wednesday, following the ritual of years, Piraí came and went. He received a few patients, almost never saw his children, and hardly ever talked to his wife. Dona Maria Augusta no longer waited for him, anxious and passionate. Wednesdays, Tuesdays, Thursdays, Fridays, they all became the same day for her, with no changes in routine except her resentment with her husband's foolishness, a man incapable of understanding the modern world.

The family was shattered. The girls came to visit, but never on Wednesdays. They came to see their mother on Sundays, late afternoon, when the husbands dozed off in front of the television after so much beer and football. Paulo José never returned from California. After the master's degree, he finished his doctorate, got married, became an American citizen and the father of two blonde boys with big blue eyes, who had never heard of Honório Gurgel and much less of phytotherapy. Pedro Tiago specialized in nuclear medicine and moved to São Paulo, where he met an heiress from a traditional family—a good reason, he thought, to hide the existence of his suburban family. João Lucas moved to the interior of Minas, where he painted the old cave inhabitants who sent him apocalyptic messages. The family, so close in the past, was now reduced to Jecé. And even he was about to lose his patience.

Disappointed with Piraí—who was nothing but a travelling salesman, old-fashioned and without culture—Jecé graduated in computer science, but science was not enough for him. Jecé inherited from his father a humanistic inclination, a generous impulse to help others. During his spare time, he taught the street children to use computers; one step towards a job, even though it would be badly paid. Teaching them, he understood that all they needed was a Piraí to support them, love them, give them direction.

His heart ached, and it was still Sunday, Palm Sunday—when he was a child, Piraí used to declare that from that day on nobody would eat meat. The memories returned, memories of his siblings playing and laughing, his mother showing all her happiness in her face. So, Jecé made a decision: he would talk to his father, even if he needed to search the whole world. He would ask for his forgiveness, thank him for his joyous childhood, a result of the heroic efforts of the man who only thought about his children and worked ceaselessly.

Determined to find his father—there was nothing in this world a website search could not find in a matter of seconds—Jecé opened his laptop and keyed Piraí's name in. The answer came quickly and the consequences were swift.

A little dizzy and in total disbelief, scared, astonished, feeling hatred for the executioner and the pain of the sentenced, not understanding the emotions in his panicked heart, Jecé jotted down an address and left the house in a hurry. He needed to see, to get the proof in person. In his hurry and despair, he did not remember to turn the computer off. Looking for her son in the bedroom, Dona Maria Augusta saw the website of the Archdioceses of Rio de Janeiro on the screen. Among the hundreds of priests registered in the State, her eyes found the name of her husband: Waldemar Lopes Piraí de Souza, pharmacist and Franciscan priest, vicar of the parish of Five Holy Wounds, in Nova Iguaçu, Baixada Fluminense.

Piraí never came home, not even on the following Wednesday, when Dona Maria Augusta's funeral took place. On Sunday afternoon, after talking to Jecé and hearing the news—among the many terrors that crossed her mind, there was the terrible threat of being a mother to werewolves, children of priests and women, as the legend said—she felt dizzy and fainted on the bed. Myocardial infarction, the doctor said, emphasizing the seriousness of her condition:

"There is no hope."

Dona Maria Augusta waited two days to die. She had become addicted to the thrill of waiting for Wednesdays.

Thursday

"It does not matter where you are; every Thursday is sex day, with no excuses or delays," warned Maria Alice, a typical South Zone carioca, owner of a perfect body sculpted by the daily hours of workouts and tanned skin; she wore the modern outfits and had the sensual gestures of those who walked through life as if they are sauntering towards the beach. That was great news for the recently married João Fernandes, who worked as an airline pilot and was therefore unable to maintain a routine, to have the calm certainty of a bureaucratic job.

During the honeymoon, followed by some vacations, the Thursday sex was not a problem. On the contrary; with the infallible competence of one able to save a burning Boeing, João Fernandes checked his instruments, had his engines in full throttle and aimed at the sky. At cruise speed and going through serious turbulence, the pilot could fly for hours without losing any fuel. Maria Alice was delighted; she had never imagined she would choose an aviation ace to marry.

But everything good has an end; that is everyone's bur-

den. When the paradise days were over, the young couple returned to their apartment in Gávea, with a view of Corcovado,
bought with the combined salaries and hard work of the two.
Maria Alice said she owned the door handles, the keys and
the bidet; her salary was very low and her paycheck was always late. In a twist of fate, she had been born with the gift of
music. She was a proud violinist in the Brazilian Symphony
Orchestra.

Maria Alice played the instrument as if a crazy angel
inhabited her hands; but she still wanted to develop her skill,
to improve her technique, to learn the violin's subtleties and
become a virtuoso. Why not? Life had been good to her. Her
parents had always stimulated her artistic vocation, and she
had married a man who admired her talent and gave her a
luxurious lifestyle. If she had to make her living with her artist's heart, she would be in hell; her impoverished country did
not have the gentleness of loving the rare ones who had a true
talent for erudition.

Her husband loved her. Returning to his daily routine,
he was in a deep panic, constantly fearing to be scheduled to
fly on Thursdays, the holy sex day. Trying to avoid the fact that
would fatally happen sooner or later, João Fernandes looked
for a religion that would honor Thursdays—the Brazilian Con-
stitution granted the people the right of having any beliefs; he
would convert and ask the airline for the weekly day of rest.
It would be a relief; he would please Maria Alice and not live
in anguish, devoured by jealousy, flying with his heart in his
throat. Believing in his idea, João Fernandes imagined himself
arguing with the Personnel Department manager: "You have
to understand. Thursdays are my holy days. If I don't honor
them, I will be cursed and reincarnate in South America again
and again, every time in a poorer country, until I finish the

cycle. Then I will be reborn as a llama in Bolivia and face the serious risk of becoming a poncho. Please help me. I will fly Saturdays and Sundays, even on New Year's Day and Christmas. But never on Thursdays." The speech was rehearsed *ad nauseam.*

Fearful they would think he was crazy and force him to retire, João Fernandes decided to remove the llama thing from the speech —that really sounded like a madman's argument—but added Dalai Lama quotes to the monologue, only to remove them as well: if they asked him anything about Buddhism, he would not be able to answer with a simple comma. He tried Oxóssi, Shiva and the Reverend Moon, and never found a convincing argument. There was not one single religion that honored Thursdays. Every Christian faith respected Sundays; the Jews honored Saturdays; the Muslims, Fridays. Candomblé, Umbanda, Buddhism, Hinduism, Taoism, Syncretism—my God, there was nothing; not even the Universal Church of the Kingdom of God had foreseen Maria Alice's idea and honored Thursdays.

A divine light came upon the head of the tormented husband. If Thursday could be sex day, so could Friday. After all, he thought hopefully, what difference can 24 hours make to the sweet violinist with the heart of a tramp? That's it; problem solved. He would convert and become a Muslim, despite the drawbacks. He would be circumcised and call himself Abdullah. Many people would be distressed boarding a plane flown by an Arab—a sign of the times—but whenever he flew to New York, he would use the good old name of Captain Fernandes. He sighed in relief. Where there is goodwill, there is no problem too difficult to solve.

When you reach an agreement, of course. Maria Alice, however, did not seem willing to cooperate. When she heard her husband's proposal to postpone sex from Thursday to Friday, because he would convert to Islam, her pretty eyes grew large:

"Changing sex day? Over my dead body. Do you think this is easy? Listen, João, people have commitments, it was difficult to organize our schedules. I cannot disturb my partners' lives just because you have suddenly decided to become a Muslim. I won't change anything.

Partners? Abdullah João Fernandes felt like he was on an airplane falling through the sky, without a single instrument to help him recover control. He had been trained to keep a level head, though, and answered the crazy woman without raising his voice:

"How many people participate in the sex day? If it isn't just the two of us, you'd better rename your Thursdays: the correct name is gang-bang." That said, he exited, slammed the door and went to a bar to drown his sorrows—a bar, the safe harbor for those who cannot see the obvious or see too well. He drank too much and came back home stumbling. João found his beloved sleeping like an angel, with the peaceful expression of those with a clear conscience. He thought about murdering her, remembering in a panic that it was Tuesday night. He would be flying on Friday. What would happen on that fateful Thursday? Anguished, he looked at Maria Alice, her tousled hair spread over the pillow, and caressed her face, gently, passionately. He stopped at her neck, and wanted to strangle her:

"Low-class bitch. God, how I love her."

He fell asleep sobbing, lost in the infamous dead-end of suspicion, hoping his wife would give up, see the logical evidence that well-married ladies do not participate in orgies—much less orgies scheduled in advance. Life is unforgiving, though. João Fernandes woke up with Maria Alice's voice on the phone:

"João only flies tomorrow. There's no chance of sex when he's at home. We'll make up for it later."

Captain João Fernandes, admired and respected for his cold competence, a man who had landed a Jumbo in adverse conditions, zero visibility and faulty landing gears without hurting the fly which had embarked accidently in Rio, did not know his beast side. Still half-asleep, a little blind, a little dizzy, he attacked his wife. He took the telephone from her hand, insulted the interlocutor on the other side of the line and hung up violently. He shook the astonished spouse, screaming like a madman:

"Who the hell do you think I am? A fool? The idiot who pays for your libertine ways? You are nothing but a second-rate violin player who lives like a princess because of my money. This is over. No more sex. Not this Thursday, not ever. Never again. Are you listening? Bitch!"

Cornered against the wall, Maria Alice started to cry. "João, have you gone mad?"

No. He had not gone mad, he was in his perfect mind, and he warned her again, clearly and slowly, that she had to forget about the Thursday bacchanal. From that moment on, Maria Alice's sex was the exclusive property of Captain João Fernandes—called Abdullah by his friends—any day of the week, anytime, anywhere. If Maria Alice dared to touch that damned subject once again, she was a dead woman. De-ca-pi-ta-ted, he explained, didactically.

"Any doubts, over?" He asked, using the jargon and the safe tone of voice reserved to the control towers of airports across the globe.

They did not speak to each other on Wednesday and

avoided eye contact. Maria Alice, deeply hurt, grabbed her violin and started playing Bomtempo's Requiem, with long arches of infinite solitude. João, enraged and touched, heard his wife's lament. Before sunset, love and music had buried the first fight. They clung to each other, in bouts of passion. Thursday came, and was spent as had been expected; sex all day long. Whatever João created, the tireless Maria Alice returned with stronger desire. They did not have lunch or dinner, fed only by the flesh that made two become one, always wanting more, wanting death, the absolute orgasm of those who love without measure. Exhausted and happy, João Fernandes woke up and went off to the airport to fly a jet plane with three hundred passengers.

If was a perfect flight, safe as it could be. Exhausted, happy, satisfied, flirting with the cloudless sky and reliving every moment of the previous day in his mind, João Fernandes suddenly understood that the Thursday problem had not been solved yet. Far from it. Now, he knew Maria Alice, the consummate cynic; she did not argue, she pretended to be submissive, but she did exactly what she wanted. Calmly evaluating the emergency in question, Captain Fernandes concluded that his recent nuptials had an engine failure. His rage would not change his wife's mind or her decision to have sex every Thursday. Thinking better, he had made a mistake. Captains do not lose their heads and start screaming like he had. On the contrary, they assess the problems and face them with elegance—whenever possible, of course; normally the Captain's charm has already disappeared when the airplane explodes.

João had the sad sensation that he was flying a marriage without chance of rescue; a cold despair ran down his spine. What would Maria Alice be doing at that exact moment? Would she be having sex? With whom? Where? The damned woman knew he would not come back before Saturday night; she could indulge herself in each and every delight, even using the marital bed with a view of Corcovado… what a whore, my God.

Jealousy is the twin brother of delirium. Unable to control his nerves, João Fernandes tried to visualize his potential rival: would he be the thin orchestra conductor, with his captivating smile? The tall bass player? The pianist with light hands? The tenor who could produce a do that she admired? The building's garage attendant? João Fernandes imagined every single one of them in his wife's arms. He felt nauseated. A thick, cold sweat soaked his shirt collar, and he had to loosen his tie. The copilot, Heraldo Ambrósio, noticed his discomfort:

"Is everything alright?"

"I'm just feeling a little sick. I've probably had something off."

Indeed, he had…his wife. Now, she was twisting his guts, planting a pair of horns on his head, and he refused to feel the pain of the betrayed, drowning in anguish, a pulsing suffering with no relief. Without thinking, he spoke too loud:

"It hurts too much."

"Where does it hurt, Fernandes? You look awful!"

At that precise moment, João Fernandes imagined the tenor who could sing a high do producing the lyrical note after reaching an orgasm with Maria Alice. The sound reverberated in his head and perforated his ears, awakening a sudden rage in the man. Irritated, he told his copilot to go to hell and ignored the first contact from Buenos Aires' control tower, greeting the Brazilian flight and giving him the coordinates of approximation and landing.

Unable to think—in his head, the tenor did not stop

screaming with passion—João Fernandes disconnected from the world. The poor traffic controllers in Buenos Aires suffered the consequences:

"Buenos Aires, flight 4378. Please, stop bothering me. The day is clear and bright, I will land as I please. Get the other aircrafts out of my way because my plane has lost brakes. Over."

"Flight 4378, what is your emergency? Over."

"All sorts of emergencies, *mi Buenos Aires querida*. My wife has been kidnapped, the left engine has exploded, the right engine has stopped, the flaps are stuck and I have diarrhea. Do you want to hear more? Over."

"Flight 4378, please specify the damages and keep calm. We will bring you safely to the ground. Over."

"Buenos Aires, my name is Abdullah. I don't think you can help me. I have a lyric singer residing in my head, but leave things to me, I will kill him and I will land this plane. Over."

Panicking, Heraldo Ambrósio tried to take the controls, but João Fernandes pushed him away and looked at him with the cold, calm logic of maddened people:

"If you want to stay alive, be quiet. Do as I tell you or I will throw this damned plane on the ground. Would you like to see that?"

He pointed the nose of the aircraft to the ground and started a steep descent. He leveled the plane soon after, taking pity on Ambrósio's horrified expression and the desperate screams of the three hundred passengers. Before the flight attendant could come into the cockpit to see what was happening, João Fernandes told the copilot to lock the door. While he was doing so, Fernandes commented off-handedly that he hated lyric singers:

"The one who took over my brain cannot stop singing.

What potent lungs the son of a bitch has! But after coming like he did…Too bad my lungs do not match my pleasure."

Ambrósio thought he could take advantage of the calm moment:

"Fernandes, give me the controls."

"Fuck off. Do you think I would give the controls of my plane to someone called Ambrósio? Someone with such a name shouldn't even pull a rickshaw."

Happy with the insult, he turned on the communication button: "Ladies and gentleman, this is Captain Abdullah speaking. I am a Muslim fundamentalist and member of Hamas. We have just started our landing procedures, and will arrive soon at the Buenos Aires Airport. I have no idea about the local temperature and couldn't care less. It's probably cold. It won't be a smooth landing, I forgot my glasses at home. But the copilot Ambrósio, who is scared shitless, will help me try to find the runway. If the tenor who fucked my wife and now insists on screaming inside my head stops bothering me, we will be on the ground within minutes. One way or another, because we have run out of fuel. Thank you for choosing our airline and fuck you all."

All hell broke loose in the cabin. Buenos Aires told the world that a Brazilian jetliner, hijacked by an Arab terrorist named Abdullah, was about to crash over the Casa Rosada, 9/11-style. While João Fernandes scared his crew and passengers with radical maneuvers, the world press invaded the Argentinian airport and the headquarters of the airline in Rio de Janeiro. American press correspondents did not take long to discover that Captain Abdullah, an Iraqi engineer who had received a doctorate degree in Germany, had obtained his flying license at the Jacarepaguá Airport. He was a brave man who was renowned for his aeronautical skills and used to go hang-gliding every weekend, come rain or shine. By the way, as the CNN anchorman said, his sports colleagues had always found Abdullah's introspective manners weird, as well as his strange habits of paying everything in cash. Abdullah used a 10-dollar bill to pay for a humble ice cream. The Brazilian Association of Hang-Gliding, cornered by the international news agencies, issued an official statement saying there was nobody called Abdullah among their members.

Such statements gave a lot of ammunition to the paranoids. The CIA declared immediately that the Brazilian Association of Hang-Gliding had been under investigation for months, due to suspicions that it sheltered a Muslim terrorist cell. Actually, as a secret agent declared in Washington, the takeoff platform in Pedra Bonita—a location with one of the most beautiful views of Rio—was a front. The hang-gliders took off from there just to hide the fact that there was a clandestine radio station under the platform, sending orders to the Shiite actions in Middle-East.

"Captain Abdullah is the manifested, flying evidence of this tropical conspiracy. We will not be fooled again."

Journalists are restless creatures. The American had just finished his statement when a TV station in Rio discovered the address of the apartment in Gávea and sent a news crew there. Maybe the Captain's wife—the reporters had also found out about Maria Alice's musical talents—could get in touch with her husband, calm him down, give him some support; convince the Iraqi madman that Brazil is a peaceful country which hates to get involved in foreign troubles. They did not find her, though:

"She's just left for sex," said the maid, delighted because she was on TV.

"What is sex? Where can we find her?" Asked the reporter with a malicious smile.

"Ah, mister, I don't know. Dona Maria Alice left bathed in perfume, carrying her violin case. She said she wouldn't be back for dinner."

The news was quickly broadcasted all over the world and new versions appeared in different languages. Some people affirmed that a nymphomaniac violinist, expert in tantric sex, had seduced the Captain and hijacked the plane. The Buenos Aires control tower did not take long to give the news to the pilots:

"Flight 4378, maintain your levels of speed and altitude. Mr. Abdullah, do not do anything crazy. We will meet your demands. Are there any wounded passengers on board? We want to speak to Captain Fernandes."

"I am Captain Fernandes, you idiot. I'm also called Abdullah. What do you want now?"

"Terrorist Abdullah, we have control of the situation. Tell the Captain that we have tried to talk to his wife, but we couldn't find her, she went to a session…"

João Fernandes could hear laughing and jokes when the traffic controller, without turning the radio off, asked his colleague in a low voice:

"*Qué es lo que hace realmente la señora Fernandes en las tardes de los viernes?*"

"Sex?" Asked another male voice in the Buenos Aires tower, breaking into laughter.

It was too much humiliation for poor João Fernandes, a hot-blooded male. Distressed with the public betrayal of his wife—God, he loved her so much, he had been willing to offer himself in surgical sacrifice, be circumcised and become a Muslim, never fly on Fridays, stay by her side—João Fernandes lost his last neurons. Taken by a sudden desire of revenge, of hurting the shameless woman—that whore would spend the rest of her life as the one responsible for an aeronautical tragedy—Fernandes talked to his passengers again:

"Ladies and gentlemen, this is Captain Abdullah. I am a suicide bomber and I am going through a marital crisis. If my wife thought her adulterous sex would never have consequences, she was sadly mistaken. The world will know that she was fucking around while I worked to support her luxurious lifestyle. Now, please, fasten your seat-belts. You may drink and smoke as you please, because I am going to explode this thing. Thank you for your attention."

He did not even stop to breathe and called the Buenos Aires tower:

"Buenos Aires, this is flight 4378. For your information, you shitty little Argentinians, Friday afternoon sex is the specialty of your mothers, you *cabrones, maricones, mijones, cujones, sifones, veadones, ladrones, peidones, cagones, putones....*"

Distracted, trying to remember words to continue insulting the traffic controllers in a strange mix of Portuguese and Spanish, João Fernandes did not notice the brave Heraldo Ambrósio coming closer and hitting him violently on the head. It was a swift gesture: João Fernandes immediately fainted. In the copilot's skillful hands, the huge jetliner landed safe and sound, among the tears and applause of the 300 passengers, who deplaned quickly while the horrified Ambrósio faced dozens of weapons pointed at his head. Convincing the Argentinian army that his name was not Abdullah and he had never lived in Gávea was as difficult as the terrible moments shared with that psychotic Captain. A brave man from the Northeast, Heraldo Ambrósio did not forgive his colleague:

"Even to be a cuckold you need to be competent. If that had happened to me, I would have killed that tenor before the damned man could stain my honor."

"*Donde está el Tenor? Quién usa el pseudónimo Tenor? Quién es el Tenor?*" Asked a secret agent who looked like Carlos Gardel and had the delicate gestures of a T-Rex.

That was an unfortunate comment, concluded Heraldo Ambrósio, whose only knowledge about the tenor was that he was fucking Maria Alice, the wife of João Fernandes, the knocked-out pilot. Explaining such a simple thing cost him two teeth, a black eye and lots of random injuries. It was only after the Brazilian government interfered that the agents were convinced of Heraldo's heroism. He was commended in Argentina, applauded in Brazil, cheered by the world. Ambrósio received tributes everywhere, even in Beijing, China. He spent his vacations there, as the special guest of a hotel manager who was married to a Brazilian woman. Being famous is wonderful: blessed tenor and blessed adultery, said the copilot.

"She fucked, but we came," he said to his wife while the enamored couple went on a rickshaw ride. Meanwhile, poor João Fernandes, after spending two days totally doped in a hospital in Buenos Aires, was transferred back to Rio de Janeiro, forbidden to fly and forced to go through a severe psychological evaluation. Ashamed and saddened, he had to suffer with the embarrassment of meeting Maria Alice, who had been picked up from sexual tryst by a TV crew.

And what sex…After raiding the entire city, the reporter had finally found the discreet, well-behaved wife in the house of another violinist who played for the Brazilian Symphony Orchestra, rehearsing Brahms string sextet, Opus 18, B-flat. Besides the hostess and the center of the world-class mess, there were two violists and two cellists. For years, every Thursday, the sextet—which the musicians called Sex, in a private joke—rehearsed a new piece of music until they reached perfection, and the details of its beauty overflowed in each note: "This is what to be an artist means: the constant desire of transcending yourself," Maria Alice explained to the crowd of journalists, worried sick about her husband. "My João has gone mad? This is impossible—it's Buenos Aires' tower that's mad and that show-off of a copilot. Just wait, all will be explained."

Love is really beautiful. Even after she was told the details of the story, even after she heard the horrible words her husband had used and the news scandal questioning her honor, despite the global discussion—had she fucked or not?—Maria Alice supported her partner without feeling intimidated. She protected him from the press, accompanied him to all the testimonies of the inquest, and waited for him outside the psychiatrist's office, attentive and affectionate. She convinced her Sex partners to call off the rotation. Since the episode of João's madness, the musicians changed the rehearsal place every week. Ah, the delicate soul of those who make art!

Augusto, one of the cellists, came weekly from Niterói without complaining, carrying his huge instrument. For an entire year, the Sex group met at the apartment in Gávea, without missing one Thursday. João was enchanted by the new friends who accepted him as an equal, despite the fact that the only music he knew were the pornographic versions of Carnival songs. They were gentle and solicitous, and sometimes João watched the rehearsals, relaxed, with his eyes closed, touched by the beauty he had never known. There was a lot of eroticism involved, by the way; the musicians sat in a semicircle, and seemed to almost reach orgasm, with those ecstatic expressions on their faces, happy to accompany one another in the magical beauty of the scores. João did not care; he had learned how to respect the metaphysical pleasure that defines an artist.

On some days, however, João preferred to stay away and leave the sextet alone; but he always felt ashamed of his insane attitude, doubting the loyalty of Maria Alice, the best friend and lover a man could ever have, and ruining his own future. The rumor in the company was that he would be forced to retire. The reason? He was psychologically incapable. *God damn it*, growled João, hating himself. *I have thrown my career away.*

But his past absolved him. After exhaustive psychiatric evaluations, the airline decided to give him another chance. After all, with the exception of the absurd flight to Argentina, Captain Fernandes had an exemplary record; he was a responsible, competent, polite and brave pilot, who had faced serious emergencies twice without letting the passengers know. Therefore, they decided to allow him to go back to work. First, flying cargo planes, and then on the route Rio de Janeiro-São Paulo. Finally, three years after the event—at that point João was able to whistle the Dvořák sextet, having become a frequent participant in Sex—he found his destiny: to fly a huge jetliner. He thanked God for his countless privileges every time he boarded the plane: he was a respected professional again; his head was back in the right place; his feelings were controlled; he had a perfect marriage; and, to make things better, there was an heir on the way. Only those who truly love know happiness, Captain Fernandes used to say to his relatives, friends and crew, as well as to the Sex musicians; and when he felt overjoyed to the point his chest was about to explode, he said that to his passengers, too.

He was living in peace again. When he was not flying on Thursdays, he accompanied his wife to the Sex rehearsals; he had become an addict. He had learned to love music, and especially liked another string sextet, Brahms' Opus 36. After the rehearsal, the couple usually dined out. At the end of the night, if desire commanded, they loved each other happily with the unmatched pleasure of a trusting, good love. In short, everything was normal again.

"This is a good life," he said, stretching his muscles while the plane taxied after landing in London. It had been a year, he was flying transatlantic routes.

"Why didn't your wife come? We've all brought our families. Are you going to spend New Year's Day alone? Don't you want to come with us?" Asked the copilot, checking the instruments.

João Fernandes looked at his colleague and gave him a friendly smile: "Maria Alice didn't come because New Year's Day is a Thursday, and Thursday is Sex day. My wife won't give up Thursday Sex, even to come to Europe."

The copilot was astonished. Captain Fernandes laughed heartily: "She's a violinist with the Brazilian Symphony Orchestra and member of a string sextet called Sex. The group rehearses every Thursday. Did you know that a string sextet is one of the most difficult things to play? The members of the group are special people, angels who speak a language we mere mortals don't even understand. Thanks for the invitation, but I'll spend New Year's Day in bed, dreaming of my angel."

João Fernandes's little angel also spent New Year's Day in bed, looking at the Corcovado mountain. But she was with Augusto. The pair had fallen madly in love while João was in treatment after his Argentinian madness. If she could stand the husband's illness—he was always irritated, upset, jealous—she owed that to the cellist, who had an incredibly well-proportioned instrument. Augusto had been tireless, helping her whenever he could, and life rewarded him. The child Maria

Alice was expecting could not be João's, she said:

"We made our baby on a special Thursday. João had flown to Rome and we had just finished rehearsing Brahms' 38. I will never forget; it was my fertile time. I always play the violin and life better when I'm ovulating. My darling, art is a subtlety, and only artists understand it."

FRIDAY

Maria Gertrude Cascatinha came to this world on a Good Friday, in the beginning of the last century. Everything happened so fast that her mother, in the seventh month of pregnancy, barely had the chance to lie down. The family's cook received the girl, a tiny little creature; she fit inside the hand of the accidental midwife. After the girl was born with the speed of a fast car, the maid cut the umbilical cord with the knife she was using to chop vegetables for lunch.

The uncommon birth—fast, informal and prema-ture—left a mark on the girl's character. Gertrude was never normal. To begin with, she slept for 187 nights in a shoebox. The mother fed her with a dropper and put her in the box on the bedside table. Naked. Gertrude grew up wrapped in cotton, by recommendation of her maternal grandmother, loyal to the old beliefs that premature children only survived if they did not wear clothes.

Her first bath happened when she was six months old, after the father complained that the girl had excellent health, but smelt awfully. When she got out of the bathtub—actually, the fruit bowl disinfected with alcohol—Gertrude got her first crib and started to cry. Still unable to talk, she found out in seconds that sleeping on the table was more comfortable. To tell the others about the disgrace of being removed from the beloved piece of furniture, she cried with all the force of her lungs.

After four days and four nights of infernal screaming, the mother put her back on the bedside table. As Gertrude had grown and no longer fit in the shoebox, the mother put her in a drawer, among panties and socks. Feeling cozy, the little one shut up and sealed her childhood. From drawer to drawer—in the chest of drawers, the cupboard, the dressing table, the wardrobe—she reached the age of 15, when she reluctantly agreed to sleep on the bed to save her spine from permanent damage.

Much before she stopped sleeping in the drawers, Gertrude showed a scary tendency to avoid routine. She only wore her baby clothes—lovely little things embroidered with lace and decorated with ribbons—on her first birthday. Dressed like a newborn, with a four-toothed smile, she blew the candle of her pink cake. Well, that was what her mother had planned. Actually, due to some chemical disaster, perhaps something with the aniline, Gertrude's cake was dark purple, a detail that made her paternal aunt, a big-mouthed spinster, to declare that her niece's life was probably damned.

She had hardly finished the sentence when she fell dead to the ground. She had choked on the cake. For almost seven decades, relatives talked about the child's birthday party—a child who slept in drawers and killed her enemies with a mere look. Everyone feared her. Isolated, Gertrude sought consolation in religion and went to the church so often that she ended up eloping with Saint Anthony, as we will see.

The poor unhappy girl suffered of all sorts of illnesses, even those not yet catalogued by medical science. Before her adolescence, Gertrude was a sure presence in Medical Congresses. Curious doctors poked and probed the rare specimen who had stuck a bean in her nose and actually harvested some good-quality grains; who ate porcelain roses, suffered from chronic furunculosis, had three kidneys and spent weeks without evacuating. When she did, the whole city soon knew about it, because Rio de Janeiro was caught by a shitstorm first thing in the morning.

Gertrude's surprising infantile dysfunctions continued for the rest of her life. She menstruated through her ears, the right and the left; one each month. Because of that, she needed an ear, nose and throat specialist to treat her gynecological condition. A series of fits became a scientific puzzle: the sickly virgin, like a pilgrim, visited countless medical clinics to recover from diseases she had caught, according to the doctors, from the labor knife's blade or the drawers' mold.

Defying science, Gertrude treated her gallbladder with a dentist, her neighbor; the organ was located in one of the superior molars. A neurologist had the task of healing her tendency to have fecalomas —that is, petrified feces. Her labyrinthitis disappeared thanks to an anesthesiologist. The annoying dermatitis, which made her scratch her skin to the point of bleeding, was cured by a team of urologists. A proctologist saved her from anemia, and the general practitioner played the role of psychoanalyst until he committed suicide, exhausted after hearing Gertrude say so much nonsense—normally, sentences mixed with advertisement jingles. The poor man had no choice but doing something extreme; in his farewell letter, he expressed his anguish for being unable to interpret the daily words of the crazy patient —something like "Hallowed be God's name, the One who comes down softly,[10] or will one day."

The excess of her maladies and the disconnection of her neurons made Gertrude's parents arrive to the sad conclusion that she would not live long. Well, she surprised them in that aspect, too. Gertrude escaped any logic, and frankly, nobody would dare to support her. Despite the fact that she was well-born, well-raised and well educated, coming from a moneyed and vain clan, she never occupied herself with bourgeois details. She wore whichever clothes were handier, inside out or back to front; it did not matter—she just needed to cover herself. She wore random colors, leaning towards flashy ones. Her fashionable outfit was completed by a hat which almost covered her eyes.

If the eccentric looks were all, the Cascatinha family would coexist with their heiress without fear or anxiety. But things were not that easy. Since early childhood, Maria Gertrude gave them unimaginable scares. If her intestines, constantly blocked by fecalomas, showed a desire of getting rid of the detritus, Gertrude did not flinch. She left her stinky matter wherever she was—just to complain immediately afterwards, pointing at the mess and screaming: "What a filthy place! I don't want to stay here!"

And she would leave, lifting her chin. A faint smell of crap, which she ignored, denounced her; but she had emptied her guts and that was reason enough to feel happy. On the other hand, urinating was not a problem for her; in the middle of a party, without losing her smile, Gertrude would release the product of her three kidneys, usually producing a small

---

10 *"Aquele que desce redondo"*—reference to a popular beer advertisement in Brazil.

lagoon. To complete the strange picture, Maria Gertrude Cascatinha, a rare specimen, had exactly 64 teeth, twice the regular number: "God has made me carefully; if I break a tooth, I always have a spare one."

With such a résumé, it was not a surprise that her parents and siblings never took her seriously, except by her madness and her faith. When it was time to pray, Gertrude changed; she reached a state of transcendence. Some relatives and friends saw the sign of sanctity in the singular Gertrude; her mother, however, was not among those. A practical creature, Dona Adelaide summarized her daughter without measuring words:

"There are the mad and the saints. That's why there are asylums and churches. Gertrude goes to church, but she should be in an asylum. She's stark, raving mad since she was born."

After putting the girl into drawers so often, however, her father ended up believing she was blessed and miraculous. He proved his point of view with an irrefutable argument:

"Maria Gertrude is a celestial being. She has her liver where one of the lungs should be. This is a disturbing fact and makes her totally ubiquitous."

Ignoring the discussion and dressed like a scarecrow, Gertrude went to church daily. Come rain or come shine, she attended the Holy Mass every day, at eight o'clock in the morning—except on Sundays, holidays and Fridays, when she said the rosary, praying to the Sacred Heart of Jesus, late afternoon. She had said the rosary so many times that she probably had acquired indulgences to last for her next hundred incarnations. Whoever saw her praying, contrite, intense and pious, commented that on her knees Gertrude seemed to shine with a divine light:

"It's a resplendent wonder. You almost forget she's wearing wacky clothes."

Between her reputation as a lunatic and her fame as a divine envoy, Gertrude started to age. She was pushing thirty when, on a Friday afternoon, came back from church with a smile that barely fit her face—well, no mouth in this world can accommodate so many teeth. Dona Adelaide noticed her happiness immediately:

"What happened? Have you seen an apparition?"

"Even better," sighed Gertrude, romantically. "Saint Anthony smiled at me and then winked. I thought I was dreaming. But then he whispered that I am irresistible. He asked me out."

The mother heard the absurd words in terror. She concluded, in despair, that Gertrude's brain had finally succumbed and could never be fixed again. She was a step away from electroshock therapy. Scared, she decided to save her daughter, forcing her to think as normal people do. But mothers are always mothers. They are insistent beings, with a postgraduate in emotional blackmail.

"Gertrude, please. You have already made one doctor kill himself with your weird talk. For the love of God, spare your poor mother. Do you really want me to believe that a chalk statue has asked you out? Don't you think it's enough to defecate in public? Now you have decided to say that Saint Anthony is flirting with you! Take it easy, child, you will end up killing me. I'll die of fear and shame."

Without a murmur, and keeping her lovesick air, Gertrude locked herself in the bedroom and only left the following morning, dressed in orange, with a straw hat and flowers falling over her eyes. To complete the outfit, there were rubber flip-flops. When she walked by her mother, who was having breakfast in the kitchen, she just made one comment:

"I'm going to meet Saint Anthony. Don't I look pretty?"

Gertrude did not wait for an answer; she simply slammed the door and disappeared. She came back late at night, blissfully happy, not caring a bit about her worried parents, who thought she could have had an accident. The distressed sister even suggested the horrible possibility that Gertrude had been mistaken for one of the new garbage cans placed in the streets:

"They are bright orange. The police could have taken her to a dumpster. God, what a tragedy!"

There was no tragedy after all. Gertrude was exuding happiness. She showed her family her straw hat, crumpled after so many hugs and kisses, the proof of Saint Anthony's passion for her:

"I knew there must be a reason, a good reason, why people call him the saint of marriage. What a man, my God, what a man. I mean, what a saint. I mean, I don't know. All I know is that we are in love and we will get married."

"Who would have imagined? Fernando de Bulhões y Taveira de Azevedo, the popular Saint Anthony, tried so hard that he actually had his martyrdom after centuries: a *sui generis* spouse. The world press will have a ball publishing pictures of Mrs. de Pádua defecating in the middle of Vatican City, in the churches, in the convents and while visiting the Pope. Poor man, it would have been better to be decapitated in Morocco, as he had intended," said the annoyed mother— thinking about having Gertrude committed.

A thought she kept entertaining for the next few days. Even the father agreed that it was impossible for his daughter to continue the charade of being engaged to a statue, a symbol of a Catholic saint, worshipped and respected. In Gertrude's mind, however, that statue housed the soul of a man who waited for her every day after Mass, when they would exchange solemn vows of love. Anthony, she said—already forgetting her future husband's title—was enchanted. He could not stop praising her beauty, her intelligence, her distinct elegance; she was the bride he had been waiting for the last 800 years. Gertrude would lose her breath telling the details:

"This is nothing. We are fooling the vicar. We chose Fridays to meet so nobody would suspect. At the end of the rosary, he jumps from the altar, hugs me, and we disappear together."

The delirium was so extreme that the family was alarmed. The clan was totally lost when a local newspaper published the unexpected photograph: Gertrude, hugging a young man looking exactly like Saint Anthony—the same face, the same robes, even the halo was there. The subtitle commented, on this fashion of the times—it was the 60's, in the 20th century, where eccentricity was the rule: "The hippie-boutique fashion exaggerates in bad taste. The girl is a horror of colors and the lad defies the Church, wearing Saint Anthony's robes."

The news fell like a bomb on top of the Cascatinha family. The patriarch—always discreet, polite, self-controlled—almost had a heart attack. The sister's husband had a fit of laughter. The brother huffed and puffed:

"Who is this deceitful bastard?"

"He's Saint Anthony himself, have more respect when you talk about your brother-in-law, he's a very important man. Didn't I tell you I love Saint Anthony and he loves me back? You should get used to it; I'm going to marry him."

In the midst of all that confusion, Dona Adelaide was the only one able to keep her composure. She had decided to call the cardiologist and lock Gertrude in a madhouse. But in Gertrude's life, nothing was easily solved. During the following week, each and every doctor the family sought refused to intervene, saying they were afraid, after the GP's suicide. Dona Adelaide and Mr. Cascatinha walked their *via crucis:* cardiologist, pediatrician, orthopedist, lung specialist, surgeons, and even an expert in prostate illnesses—a longtime friend of Mr. Cascatinha's. Even the psychiatrist was consulted, but nobody accepted the mission of accompanying Gertrude to the asylum.

Watching the commotion that intended to remove her from public life for at least a few months, Gertrude fell into despair. She argued with her father, her mother, her siblings. She defied them, enraged, a true heroine who had her love put into question. She was not satisfied with insulting them, she actually made a scandal.

"I will elope with Saint Anthony if I need. I will not live without him."

"Don't forget to take an umbrella, Saint Anthony is of a weakened health," advised her brother.

Feeling sorry for the poor girl in the middle of that mess, the sister-in-law tried to help. Trying to calm Gertrude down, and the parents-in-law as well, she remembered there was an infallible medicine for excited nerves—money. She started to remind them that Saint Anthony was in the payroll of the Brazilian Army.

"Let's control ourselves. I think Gertrude will marry wonderfully well. Saint Anthony is a captain, you know? It will be hard to convince the priests, who control his paycheck, to give up the money, but the couple will live comfortably after that. Military men are not rich, but they don't starve. Why aren't we optimistic?"

She would have continued to say absurdities if her husband's fury had not interrupted her:

"Isn't one madwoman enough in the family? Have you lost your mind too? Shut the hell up before Gertrude starts thinking that her fictitious fiancé is a veteran of the Paraguayan War. What the hell is going on, anyway? Have we all gone mad?"

The brother-in-law interfered, the sister shed tears, and the father had a fit and ended up in the hospital. The maids made fun of the situation, discussing the best way to address Anthony—Doctor or Saint? The neighbors gave their two cents too, as well as distant relatives, who felt they had the right to give their opinion on the matter. The mother was so distressed and ashamed, she broke all the fine china and the crystal glasses in the kitchen, throwing the objects against the wall.

A week before Gertrude's likely commitment, the entire Cascatinha clan officially lost their heads—with the exception of Gertrude herself, who had ignored the turmoil and walked around the house daydreaming, her head on the moon, after the recent and sudden outburst. She spent the whole day at church, leaving in the morning and only returning late at night, happy and smiling.

The catastrophe happened on a Friday morning. Feeling sorry for his longtime friend, who was still in the hospital, drugged and depending on tranquilizers to sleep—the prostate expert accepted the challenge of treating Gertrude, to honor the old friendship. He gave the news to Dona Adelaide, hired an ambulance, called a couple of strong nurses and, in case of an emergency, a black-belt jiu-jitsu champion with a cauliflowered ear and an unfriendly expression. The doctor told the man:

"If she causes any trouble, deck her. Don't hesitate; Gertrude looks fragile and likes to think she's weak, but the girl is a bull."

The SOS Health entered the house at the exact moment the bride-to-be came back from church. Despite her obvious limits, no one could contain Gertrude when she realized the prostate expert had accepted the task of separating her from her beloved. Not even joining forces the black-belt champion, the ambulance driver, the brother, the brother-in-law, the neighbors, the street warden and, obviously, the doctor were they able to stop her. Feeling cornered, Gertrude threw arms and legs, shook her hips and kicked without having a specific target. The troop was soon dispatched—no one had time to realize that Gertrude had not only become the bride of a saint, but also a *Capoeira* fighter. Not even Dona Adelaide knew that side of her daughter, who after knocking the men unconscious, faced her mother with eyes full of sadness and resentment:

"I didn't want this. I wanted to have a normal wedding, do things the right way. I didn't want to do what I'll do now—elope with my saint. You have provoked this situation. I will never come back here."

Fast as a cat, she disappeared in the night, while another ambulance arrived to attend the wounded and a nurse sedated Dona Adelaide, who was in shock and repeated the enigmatic words, "it was the vegetable knife and the drawer's mold, it was the vegetable knife and the drawer's mold, it was…" A strong dose of an IV tranquilizer shut her up. Her sister and sister-in-law had to administrate the chaos that ensued.

And what chaos. Besides the second ambulance and the hordes of curious onlookers—lots of residents of the area were blocking the street where the Cascatinha family lived—the military and civil police force came, as well as the local media. An exorcist offered his services. A heavy metal band who rehearsed in the neighborhood appeared out of the blue, looking for inspiration to compose a new rock genre, heavy-celestial-romantic perhaps. Street vendors made hefty profits and several Franciscan priests showed up at the scene to accuse the austere Cascatinha clan, especially Gertrude—who had been seen in the church shortly after the commotion—of stealing the Saint Anthony's statue—a horrid thing, made of iron and chalk in a distant suburb. It did not represent a loss to the Holy Church's assets nor had it any value to justify the drama. But it had a religious, intrinsic, metaphysical importance; it mattered to the churchgoers and its disappearance meant disrespect for the rules of the noble Archdioceses. The vicar could keep talking forever, adding more and more arguments to his accusation, but Gertrude's sister interrupted him:

"The image is the size of a man. Gertrude would never be able to carry it alone, she isn't that strong. Before we do anything else, we have to discover how and when Saint Anthony disappeared from the altar."

The following day, a Friday, the church remained closed. They needed the authorization of the Cardinal to keep it closed, because the house of God does not close down like that, but the Vatican decided to forget about the episode quickly and urgently. So, the police searched every centimeter of the church looking for clues, even the most remote ones. Nothing indicated robbery or kidnapping. The side door of the sanctuary had been opened from the inside; Saint Anthony's altar was intact, only the statue was missing. The crime scene investigators said that the trail of shoe prints on the stone stairs indicated that Gertrude had not climbed the altar, but that someone had descended from it.

With a total lack of explanations—at least logical ones—the church bought a new statue; sanctified it at a big party and closed the subject—it was way too complicated. Before any crazy rumors drove hordes of spinsters to the church after grace, the Bishop transferred the vicar to the interior of Bahia and the priests were sent to distant parishes. New shepherds arrived to oversee the sheep, many of them still excited over the strange event. The Cascatinha family took advantage of the situation and fell into silence; the press ended up forgetting the whole affair. The heavy-celestial-romantic rock music was boycotted by radio stations and the record was a total failure, so the whole thing was quickly forgotten.

Gertrude disappeared for years, during which time— she swore on the Bible – she lived maritally with Saint Anthony. It was a happy marriage until the day it unfortunately ended, since unions can end. Habit destroys everything, even saintly love. So, many years after she had abandoned the clan, Gertrude reappeared on a Good Friday, sick from head to toe, but exuding health. Reintroduced to the nieces and nephews who had grown up in her absence—enchanted by Astolfo, a medical student—she fell into the domestic routine with a natural grace, as if she had never left home.

Believe me if you can, that on the same day she returned, the priests discovered the old, lost image of Saint Anthony at the church door. The vicar locked it in the safe and did not make any mention of the strange coincidence.

The only consequence of her sudden return—besides the fact that the family had a new and unexpected member, a quiet and polite boy named Fernando who followed Gertrude everywhere and called her mother—was Astolfo's decision to leave medical school and become a Buddhist monk. The fact caused a heated argument between Gertrude and her brother, who accused her of driving her nephew insane with her constant illnesses. Gertrude, of course, did not ignore the insult:

"Astolfo is incompetent. He mistook menopause for a ruptured eardrum. He's doing better in Nepal, curing his ignorance."

And from unexpected fact to unexpected fact, Gertrude followed her destiny. Despite her constant fits and her fragile health, she is an octogenarian now. Old age made her become smaller—she is sleeping in drawers again. She is actually an old lady who deserves pity.

It was early morning when Gertrude left for church, her body still stiffened by the long night in the drawer. It was a special occasion, when Gertrude could exhibit her legendary weakness in her reacting to a mugging. Despite all her disadvantages—she was an old weak lady, who needed a cane to walk, always in little steps—Gertrude challenged the thief and nearly killed him. The people could not understand how such a fragile being could have lived so long and could understand even less the extreme agility of her movements—she kicked the assailant hard, bringing him down. The coughing lady did not have one scratch. The thief, on the other hand, is still in the hospital; he had a fractured skull, lost brain matter and suffered multiple trauma.

"Astonishing lady," said the detective who led the investigation, looking at Gertrude, sitting down and looking so small, afraid they would arrest her before she had time to pack all the 737 pills she took every day. Maria Gertrude Cascatinha was a true wonder, who had spent her whole existence suffering with the incomprehension of others.

As for Fernando, the Cascatinha family still does not let him leave the house, even though he is almost forty now. Gertrude's son transcends reality—over his head shines a light like the halo of a saint. The halo follows him wherever he goes, as if it was part of his body. According to Gertrude, Fernando makes miracles. But she is a nutcase and nobody believes her. Who would believe a woman who sleeps in a drawer and whose blood was contaminated by a vegetable knife?

SATURDAY

Many years as a police officer had earned him the privilege. Detective Aníbal Cunha dos Santos, aka Rip—a friendly nickname, short for Ripper, which he liked a lot—butchered poor bastards without hesitation or mercy. From Sunday to Friday, his colleagues could count on his help any time of the day or night; if the subject was death, they only had to call Rip, an expert in the many ways to kill someone slowly. But he never worked on Saturdays.

Despite being 70 and a chain-smoker, suffering from emphysema, there had never been a more respected killer among police officers. Everybody knew that many arrogant criminals had crapped their pants after being threatened with "a little conversation with Rip," an expression that was quickly incorporated into the jargon of all police stations in Rio. Most of the time, if the suspect was quiet and refused to confess his guilt, all it took was a phone call to Rip:

"Hey, brother, start talking fast or Rip will come and have a little chat with you."

That worked like a charm. The suspect would open

his mouth and confess even crimes his mother had not committed. It was not surprising. Aníbal Cunha dos Santos had a very impressive *curriculum vitae*. He had lost count of the bodies he carried around like a burden; and killed anyway he needed to, even legally—that is, in the course of official business, with a fatal shot in self-defence. Well, in those cases it was Detective Aníbal who pulled the trigger. Rip only made an appearance at those painful times when he needed to slowly eliminate those who had broken the law beyond limit—the swift execution of a single judge—Aníbal himself. In his private court there were no lawyers, no appeals, and no evidence—*Data venia*, if Aníbal rendered a verdict, Rip executed the sentence with no delay.

The cruel instinct had been awakened in Aníbal many years ago. He was still very young when during an investigation in a derelict area of Rio he found a woman crying inconsolably, after being raped. Despite his total lack of empathy towards the sobbing beauty, who wore a dress that revealed every line and every curve of her delightful ass—the bitch teases a man and complains afterwards?—Aníbal listened to her lament, fulfilling his duty. He thought she was responsible for her own disgrace—if a woman wants to be a tease, she has to suffer the consequences.

He was a little distracted, spacing out—his eyes were more focused on the woman's curves than his ears on her story. Suddenly, his heart skipped a beat, getting stuck in his throat. He could not believe what he was hearing. Aníbal looked at the tearful woman, raising his voice:

"Explain again, ma'am. Who has been raped?"

"My boy, my six-year-old son! They tore him apart. Oh, detective, for the love of God, help me."

Hate, helplessness, disbelief—shame for the animal that

lives in every man, that needs to be reigned in so as not to gallop away. When he saw the victim, a little helpless thing, innocence and beauty together in a pool of blood, Aníbal went mad. At that moment, the honored detective knew his bestial side, which he could not and did not want to control—Rip.

Rip and Aníbal shared the same body. Differently from Rip, however, Aníbal was known for his delicate manner: he cared for the victims of injustice with deep affection. In the many years of life of the attentive detective, his humanitarian soul had not failed one single time. Whoever he believed was the victim of a crime received much more than the police had the obligation to offer. Aníbal consoled the wounded with love and respect, and money, when necessary. A saint, some people believed. The dead boy's mother never forgot his kindness, kneeling beside the dying child, caressing his head tenderly and singing kindergarten songs until the sad moment when the innocent kid passed away.

Aníbal arrested the rapist himself. Rip made an appearance in the back of the police car and impaled the criminal with a baton. The man died of the same injuries as the little angel—he had his intestines torn and suffered internal hemorrhaging. The excuse presented to the police chief, who complained about the bloodied wreck entering his station, was that the people of the local community had taken care of the punishment:

"It is classic punishment, Chief, an eye for an eye and a tooth for a tooth. Forget about it. That scumbag got what he deserved."

Nothing came of it and Aníbal developed a secret enjoyment in playing vigilante. As time went on, killing by shooting, stabbing or suffocation no longer satisfied him—those were quick, puerile methods. After all, he believed a quick death did not avenge anything. On the contrary, it was almost a favor. Sometimes, in prison, inmates faced much worse hardships than being shot, waking up in hell.

And that was how the habit of cutting people slowly was born. First, a finger, and then another finger, an ear, the genitals—but the victim ended up fainting and did not feel the horror anymore. Rip was bored. He wanted them alive, awake, and aware. Prolonged suffering was the basic rule for any torturer, and Aníbal was a consummate professional: with his meager salary, he decided to help Rip and bought him medical books. A good academic background would teach him to keep his mutilated victims awake until the end, a great idea that Rip took advantage of. His studies of anatomy made the macabre a sophisticated art. The more he learned, the more the poor bastards suffered. During the executions, they only lost consciousness shortly before dying, a professional job. Said Rip:

"My little sheep scream a lot, until they lose their voice."

At that point, everyone in the police force knew him. He was a controversial character, loved and hated with the same intensity. People called him everything: a coward, evil, an assassin, brave, indispensable. "Three more Rips in this city and all violence would end," his admirers said. "Innocent people died in the hands of this psycho," his critics affirmed.

Friends and foes, however, had to agree that there was no colder or crueler man in this world—by any terms. The truth is that nobody knows anybody in this life. When he returned home to the old neighborhood on the border between the suburbs of Rio and the poverty of *Baixada Fluminense*, Aníbal let his third personality take control—Bibi, as Cândida, his beloved wife, who loved her amorous husband deeply, called him—a devoted father for the six children the couple had, three boys and three girls, all very polite.

Bibi was the soul of the neighborhood, the one who organized the parties. The residents of the area met so often that they ended up united in a sincere friendship—all Bibi's work. The women liked each other, sharing their problems and caring for the children of those who had to work. The men respected each other. The kids played and behaved like a group of cousins. Everyone from the surrounding areas envied the neighborhood and wanted to live there. Thanks to Bibi, who planned the afternoon meetings—he put the chairs on the sidewalk, where people would sit down for leisurely conversation—as well as the Sunday barbecues and the typical June parties. He was also responsible for buying the beer to celebrate the National Football Team's matches.

In World Cup years, Bibi started to decorate the street very early. The children tried to help, overexcited, but ended up making a mess. Bibi was patient, loved the atmosphere of excitement and proudly said that the innocence of childhood was more important than any goals. The parents laughed, grateful—it was hard to find such a solicitous neighbor and steadfast friend.

Even though they appreciated the blessed presence of the friendly cop—it ensured their safety, kept the thieves away (for they knew Rip lived around there)—the neighbors could not avoid gossiping about the astonishing fact that Bibi was a detective, for after all, the man was delicate as a flower. One more step and he would end up becoming gay. He could not even kill cockroaches. When one of the filthy insects appeared, he disappeared, explaining bashfully:

"I'm not afraid. They're just disgusting."

If nobody helped him, he had to call Cândida to kill the roach with a flip-flop. His friends laughed at the macho detective:

"Climb on top of the table, Bibi, or it will attack you. Be careful, this one is big."

Sometimes Bibi did climb the table. If the roach flew, he flew even faster, hiding behind the first door. It was only after Cândida smashed the insect with her footwear that Bibi came back to the room, while his friends booed him affectionately. Surely, this sweet man— with the name and the attitude of an angel, who depended on his wife to kill a cockroach—had just a bureaucratic job on the force.

"Oh, come on, Mr. Bibi, I cannot see you pulling a trigger, you're too good," said the old Viridiana, who owned half of the street, and had become rich thanks to the high prices of rent—that were only becoming higher, thanks to the community spirit of Aníbal Cunha dos Santos. She thanked the Lord for her rare tenant, capable of keeping the peace and at the same time bringing joy to the place with his mere presence. Therefore, Viridiana never raised the detective's rent. When he said he did not ask for nor wanted a different treatment, the landlady said:

"Your honesty is amazing. I don't treat you differently, this is business—you make the street more valuable and I charge you a lower rent. Besides, Mr. Bibi, being your neighbor is an honor and a privilege."

And so the years passed. Along with the bodies—torn apart with the victims still alive—and the neighborhood parties, Aníbal raised his children; and the killer who lived inside him became more and more cruel. Once, he was invited to spend a few days in another Brazilian state, to speed up the execution of a horrendous criminal. Rip accepted. He returned, proud of the accomplished mission—the man had suffered ten hours of agony, in one of the most perfect quartering sessions he had ever realized. The party had started at the man's tongue—the very tip of it, by the way.

Nobody knew anything at home, and Aníbal did not even remember his dirty jobs. Bibi and Cândida lived there with their beloved offspring, Bibi-style, enjoying a playful life—and the children learned the secrets of tenderness. The detective had the task of teaching them morals and ethics; respect towards other citizens; what was right and wrong. But against Aníbal's will, Rip ended up making an appearance—thanks to the curiosity of Átila, one of his sons, who never missed a chance to bury his nose in an anatomy book. Once the detective forgot one of his volumes left opened on the table. His wife got scared and he explained that studying the human body was part of his job:

"If I need to shoot, I know where to aim. You know how it is..."

Cândida was proud:

"And our friends make fun of your fear of cockroaches..."

To speak the truth, Aníbal worried about Átila's morbid curiosity. He relaxed, however, after talking to him—for the boy's dream was to study Medicine—a dream that came true. This happened for all six children of Aníbal and Cândida. All of them were grateful to their father, so sweet and tender, and all of them married well, had excellent jobs and finished university.

Time made Aníbal an enchanted and enchanting grandfather. His grandchildren adored him, and got anything they wanted from him without effort—or it would not be Bibi, as Cândida, her children, sons and daughters-in-law, neighbors and friends said about the cop with the spirit of a flower:

"Bibi is very affectionate. He can't even kill a cockroach. He could only have become this fairy-tale grandfather."

Besides the expansion of the clan, destiny award-
ed Aníbal with an extra surprise: Átila specialized in forensic
medicine. Proud and happy, the detective applauded his son's
brilliant career. The boy soon changed from an anonymous
doctor to a college professor and the Director of the Coroner's
Office. Aníbal, Rip and Bibi did not miss one chance of talking
proudly about that perfect heir, who was able to cut cadavers
with the same skill the father used to cut live bodies.

Meanwhile, the criminals sentenced to death died Rip-
style—tortured with skilful cruelty. As a father of a doctor
of forensics and a frequent witness to autopsies, Bibi made a
super-expert out of Rip, until Átila had to confess that one
needed a degree to admire him properly. He had never imagined that his father had such deep knowledge of human anatomy. Aníbal tried to change the subject:

"Don't exaggerate. I research for amusement, for sport.
You took after me, but you are the one with the knowledge,
you know the subject in depth. You're the first-class professional."

He took the opportunity to clear some doubts about the
possible consequences of castration in adult men. Átila reacted with surprise:

"Why do you want to know this? It gives me the creeps,
just to think about it."

None the less he explained everything in detail, proud
of the interest of his father in his profession. He never suspect-
ed that the information he gave triggered a period of excessive
violence. With that knowledge, Rip started to emasculate rap-
ists and pedophiles. Armed with a razor, he did the job with
extreme speed and skill. Before the intervention, he even let
the sentenced men sniff a little ether. Pain would come with
the surprise, the humiliation of knowing they were no longer

men—a punishment for life.

In the same period that he became a castration ace, Aníbal stopped working on Saturdays. He refused to retire, in spite of the insistence of his superior officers. Seeing his new colleagues, who had made it to the police force via tests and were basically a bunch of sissies, Aníbal doubted that the police could maintain the peace in the city. He still considered himself important to society—together with Rip, he had much to do. But on Saturdays he disappeared from the police station, and dedicated that day exclusively to his grandchildren.

There were fifteen children; the party started on Friday night. They went for a walk, had a picnic, went to the zoo, to the theatre, to the circus, to the beach and to the movies. As they watched their grandchildren grow up as their children had—smiling, friendly and gentle—Bibi and Cândida's happiness grew, too. The couple seemed to know the secret of eternal bliss, loving each other, giving without asking anything in return.

Aníbal, Rip and Bibi were coexisting in blessed peace when the bomb exploded right on top of their collective heads. On a Saturday morning, Bibi was kidnapped while talking to his two oldest grandsons at the bar on the corner, with the usual friends. The news spread fast, and the house filled within minutes—friends, neighbors, curious people, members of the press and some of his police colleagues, sent to investigate the crime. The team was puzzled—the crowd only had sweet words to describe Aníbal. Faced with his polite, well-raised family, who did not seem to be related to a monster like Rip, the cops kept their silence.

They only wanted to make sure and collect all possible evidence that the polite, sweet Bibi—the devoted spouse, loving father, playful grandfather, solicitous friend, a tender man who could not even kill a roach—was actually Rip—the cruellest, coldest and most sadistic police detective in Rio. Once they had come to the indisputable conclusion that Bibi and Rip shared the same life, the law enforcement men disappeared. They knew exactly what kind of fate awaited the good and gentle Bibi: death. If he had any luck, he would not suffer much.

Cândida personified the pain of those who lived with the innocent victim of that city without law—Bibi, a dedicated professional, equally careful with criminals and victims. Without hearing news of her husband, the woman's heart weakened—fearful of losing the love of her life, her greatest passion, she ended up in the hospital. The children would not leave her side, but Átila, her only doctor, dedicated every second of his day to her. He spent day and night with his mother, as his father surely would if he could.

He only left his vigil as the family doctor when, on Friday, his assistants at the coroner's office requested his presence. A week before, the police had found a body in the city, sliced as a piece of meat. There was no way they could identify the body because the fingerprints had disappeared; there was no skin left. Only a DNA test would solve the puzzle and tell them if those pieces of meat had belonged to a man or a woman. The other doctors, knowing about the director's life tragedy, did all they could not to bother him, but scientific curiosity was stronger than their feelings:

"Professor, please come. We have a singularly unique set of circumstances—you will enjoy analyzing this astonishing case. We have already searched the literature, searched the Internet—there has never been a case like this. Nothing as violent as this."

So violent that it caused deep anguish in Átila, who did

not know why it happened. While he studied the micro pieces of what had once been a human being—good or bad, it did not matter—the forensic doctor thought: What kind of animal could be capable of doing that?

The answer did not take long to come. It was almost late afternoon when one of his assistants called him, a little shaken, lowering his eyes—the coroner's office car had arrived, bringing the dead body of Aníbal Cunha dos Santos:

"Professor, they have found your father. The cops have identified the body and found Detective Aníbal's documents in his pockets. Let us deal with this, you don't need to get involved. It is a shocking scene for any son, even for a forensic doctor."

Even though he could not fathom a single thing that was happening, Átila got involved. That day had been destined to surprise him: first, a horribly disfigured body, violently dilacerated; then, the astonishing fact that the cops had found Bibi in the middle of the street, inside a coffin, amidst flowers, and without his head. The scene was so horrendous that Átila had to agree with his assistants and avoided performing the autopsy on the headless body of his father—a horror of such brutality he did not deserve.

But that surprising day had not yet ended. When Átila arrived home, the doorman gave him a gift-wrapped package—his father's head, conserved in formaldehyde. His eyes were open, as if he had been looking fearfully at his own violent, slow, macabre death. A note hanging from his left earlobe told the doctor that Rip—codename for Detective Aníbal Cunha dos Santos, the most violent monster in the entire Brazilian police force—had personally sliced up the body that had earlier shocked the coroner's office's team and that it had belonged to a young man accused of molesting little kids. The police discovered it had been a false accusation; but Rip had already killed him, cutting him into little pieces.

There were those who could not bear watching the sacrifice. But Aníbal actually had come—he had never had the pleasure of such an intense orgasm after a killing. The letter, signed "cops recently hired and disgusted" ended with the most sincere words of esteem and consideration along with a horrid post-script—Aníbal had crapped in his own pants when he faced the razor which had slowly castrated him, before expiring.

After the funeral, that happened the following morning—a Saturday morning when the grandchildren had cried for Bibi—Átila Cunha dos Santos resigned from his job at the coroner's office and started a new career: he became a police detective, just like his father.

After all, he had taken after his old man.